I'll be Home for Christmas

Kindred Spirits Mysteries

Beth Connor

WOLF GROVE MEDIA, LLC

Copyright © 2024 by Beth Connor

All rights reserved.

No portion of this book may be reproduced in any form without written permission from the publisher or author, except as permitted by U.S. copyright law.

Contents

CHAPTER ONE

Do You Hear What I Fear?

"Help me," There was a womans voice on the other end of the line.

The urgency of the request did not surprise Ashlyn Alden. It wasn't the first time someone had opened with a plea, and it wouldn't be the last. Still, she had answered the phone on a whim—usually; she let these calls go to voicemail, filtering out the pranksters, skeptics and the ones who weren't ready for help.

But today, something had nudged her to pick up. Maybe she'd been feeling bold. Maybe even adventurous. If she were honest, she had just been feeling lonely.

"Okay," Ashlyn said, her tone steady. "Start from the beginning."

"I have a ghost. She gets angry sometimes." The woman paused, her breath hitching. "I run a bed-and-breakfast, and... I'm afraid she might hurt someone."

"I'm sorry," Ashlyn began, "I don't banish ghosts. You'll probably want to call—"

"No!" the woman interrupted, her voice sharp. "Why would I want to banish her?"

Now, that was interesting. Most people wanted their ghosts gone, exorcised like yesterday's bad luck. Plenty of folks out there offered that kind of service—some genuine, others complete frauds. But Ashlyn had never been like most people.

She'd known she was different from a young age. While other little girls were dreaming of fairy tales and imaginary friends, Ashlyn was having full-blown conversations with spirits—philosophical ones, even. And not just ghosts. Ghosts were only part of the picture. There were things out there—spirits of the land, whispers of memory, old gods—that most people never noticed.

But ghosts? Ghosts were her favorite.

"How can I help?" she asked in the tone she'd perfected for these situations. Calm, kind, the voice that made people believe things would be okay.

"Vera's very sweet. I just don't know what's making her so angry."

Well. That was an unexpected twist.

Ashlyn leaned back in her chair, intrigued. "Alright. Let's go back a bit. Tell me everything."

"Well, we bought the place about five years ago when John retired," the woman began, her voice a little breathless. "John is my husband."

"Hold up," Ashlyn interrupted, balancing the phone between her ear and shoulder. "What's your name?"

"Oh! I'm sorry, dear. I'm Delores Miller. I own Lilac Grove B&B up in Laconia, New Hampshire."

"Nice to meet you, Delores. I'm Ashlyn Alden."

"Thank you, sweetie. I'm all flustered. This whole situation has me feeling like I've lost my marbles."

"Don't worry about it," Ashlyn said. "Take your time."

Delores took a moment, then started again. "Like I said, John and I bought Lilac Grove after we retired. We don't have kids, so we thought a little bed-and-breakfast would keep us busy, keep us part of the community. He does all the handyman work, and I do the cooking, cleaning, decorating—you know, the usual."

"Makes sense," Ashlyn replied, already picturing it. A cozy inn, lilacs in bloom, a perfect place for a haunting.

"We named it Lilac Grove because of the flower garden out back. There's a whole grove of lilacs—just beautiful in the spring," Delores added, her pride evident. "Anyway, we found out it was haunted almost right away."

Ashlyn straightened up. "Haunted? From day one?"

"Oh yes. The very first day. We were walking through, dreaming up our little projects, and when we stepped out into the garden. And there she was."

"Who?"

"A woman," she said, her voice dropping to a conspiratorial tone. "She was out there, tending to the lilacs in this long fur coat. Now, that didn't seem too odd at first, considering how chilly it's been that May. But then—" she paused, "she turned around, and I saw she wasn't wearing a single thing under that coat. Not one stitch."

Ashlyn stifled a laugh. "You're kidding. Your husband must have loved that."

Delores snorted into the receiver. "Oh, honey, let me tell you, he didn't know where to look. I swear, the man's eyes nearly popped out of his head. And here I am, thinking maybe I needed stronger glasses."

"That's one way to may an impression."

"We thought she might be confused, maybe one of the previous owners. But before we could say anything, she just... faded. Like smoke."

Ashlyn nodded to herself. "That's a classic one."

"Yes. After that, we'd see her now and then. She putters around and rocks in the old chair in the parlor. She's always been quiet—friendly, even. Guests love her. She's part of the charm."

"But something changed?"

Delores hesitated. "That first December, she started tearing down the Christmas decorations, knocking things over, even pushing guests. We tried talking to her, but I don't think she can hear us."

Ashlyn raised an eyebrow. "Only around the holidays?"

"Exactly! And after Christmas, she calms down. The next December, it was worse. She started a fire in one room, and a poor man almost got shoved down the stairs. We had to shut down for the season."

Ashlyn frowned. "And now?"

"We've closed for the holidays the last two years. Figured it was safest. But we can't afford to keep doing that. December's a busy month, and with everything getting more expensive..." Her voice trailed off, dropping to a worried whisper. "I'm scared of what she'll do if we stay open."

Ghosts had personalities—quirks, just like the living. Some stuck around for sentimental reasons, others for unfinished business. But this kind of pattern, escalating during the same season every year? That was interesting.

"How do you want me to help?"

"Well," Delores hesitated again. "We were hoping maybe you could talk to her? See what she wants? We don't want her gone. She's part of the place now, you know?"

Ashlyn thought it over. Spirits weren't the sort to just spill their secrets, and this would not be a simple chat. Building trust with the dead took time. Effort.

"This isn't the kind of thing that'll be fixed overnight," Ashlyn warned.

"Oh, no, no," Delores agreed. "We don't expect that. I know we probably can't afford your usual rates, but the place is empty in December. Maybe you could stay with us for the month? We'll feed you, take care of everything. I promise we'll be excellent hosts."

Ashlyn paused, considering. A cozy B&B, tucked away in New Hampshire, surrounded by snow and a temperamental ghost to figure out? She had no family to spend Christmas with, and her spirit friends weren't the caroling type. The idea of a month-long holiday away, with a supernatural mystery to solve, was... tempting.

"All right," she said, the decision made. "I'll come."

Delores' exhaled. "Oh, thank you, Ashlyn! You have no idea how much this means to us."

"I'll have my business manager get in touch to work out the details of the contract. We'll get everything squared away before I head up."

"Of course," Delores replied, her excitement clear. "Thank you. We've been at our wits' end."

"Not a problem. I'm looking forward to meeting you and seeing the Lilac Grove for myself. It sounds lovely."

"It is," Delores said. "We're proud of it. And... well, we're proud of Vera, too. She's part of the family in her own way."

Ashlyn's smile widened. "Vera, huh? I can't wait to meet her as well."

Delores chuckled, the tension easing. "Let's hope she's on her best behavior."

"We'll see," Ashlyn replied. "I'll see you soon. Take care."

"You too, sweetie."

When the call ended, Ashlyn sat back, tapping her fingers on the desk. A haunted bed-and-breakfast, a ghost with a holiday grudge, and an entire month to sort it all out?

Ashlyn had sent off an email to her business manager mid-conversation, her thumb tapping out details while

Delores rambled on about lilacs and holiday décor disasters. By the time they ended the call, Ashlyn already had one foot out the door.

Ashlyn sat at her desk, the phone still in her hand. The universe had a way of arranging things, weaving events together in patterns she didn't always recognize until later. Sometimes, it knew what she needed before she did.

Her phone buzzed, pulling her from her thoughts. It was a reply from Caroline, her business manager—quicker than usual.

Details sorted. Lilac Grove B&B, starting tomorrow. Looks like you'll be there by noon if you leave on time. They're covering meals, so don't scare them with your snack habits. C.

Ashlyn smiled at the screen. Leave it to Caroline to handle things faster than she could even plan. It was comforting, really. Caroline was a force of nature, the kind of person who could wrangle chaos with a cup of tea and a clipboard.

If she packed tonight, she'd be ready to hit the road by morning. The drive wasn't long—just a few hours—but it would give her time to think. Lilac Grove was waiting, and with it, whatever mess was brewing beneath the surface. She'd learned long ago that small towns always had trouble simmering, like a pot on a stove left too long.

Her gaze drifted to the framed photo on her desk. A little girl, five or six, standing between her parents. It was the last picture they'd taken together. Sometimes it felt like a relic from another world, proof they'd been real, because her memories were fraying at the edges. Her dad's big, warm hugs, her mom's smile—things she used to be able to recall so vividly—were growing harder to hold on to.

They'd always accepted her. Never questioning her odd little gifts, the way she'd talk about things no one else could see. And when they'd been taken from her, she'd half expected them to come back. Not alive, but... present. Lingering. Watching over her. Spirits, after all, were supposed to stick around, weren't they? The ones with unfinished business?

But they never had.

Maybe they'd moved on. That's what people said when they wanted to offer comfort. "They've found peace," they'd tell her. "They're in a better place." And maybe that was true. But it wasn't comforting. Not to her.

She exhaled, leaning back in her chair. After they'd passed, it had been foster home after foster home. Each one was more interested in her oddities than in her as a person. Some feared her abilities, whispering about devils and curses. Others saw them as something to exploit, a party trick or worse. She'd learned to keep quiet. It was easier that way.

At least her ghost friends had been more understanding. But even they didn't have answers. Not about her parents. Not about why they hadn't stayed. Ghosts didn't have all the answers. Being dead didn't make you wise, just... well, dead.

She pushed the thoughts aside. It hurt less now, in a distant, quiet sort of way—like anyone else who had lost their parents, except her holidays always had an extra twist of loneliness.

She stood, stretching her arms and glancing around her small apartment. Relationships had never been her strong suit, and she preferred to keep her friends at a comfortable distance. Alone wasn't so bad. She had her routine, her work and her friend Sebastian when she needed a distraction. That was about as close as she got to companionship. He wasn't looking for anything more, which worked for her.

Dating? Well, that was always a temporary affair. A few dates, nothing serious. She liked to keep things casual, before things got to the point where explaining the ghosts became necessary. That was usually the deal-breaker.

It didn't bother her. Some people had pets; she had a handful of spirits who dropped by for a chat.

Ashlyn gave a small shrug, shaking off the melancholic thoughts before they could settle. She had a trip to prepare for. She flicked on her laptop and opened a browser, pulling up articles about Lilac Grove. Most were puff pieces—*Charming B&B in Laconia*—filled with reviews about the delightful décor and the infamous ghost, who was known for moving guests' shoes or knocking over a teacup. But then she found an old local legend buried in the archives: Vera Beaumont had once been a woman of high society in the late 1800s, known for her hospitality.

Ashlyn would have to see what information the Millers had already dug up on her. Obviously something, as they had named her. The timeline of her life was murky—rumors of a lost child, a conspiracy with her husband, murder or worse—but nothing concrete.

"Classic," Ashlyn muttered to herself. Tragic backstory? Check. Holiday tantrum? Double check.

She leaned back, thinking through the details. It wasn't like spirits to get angry without reason, and Vera had been a benign presence for years—cheeky, sure, with her pranks and shoe-misplacing, but nothing violent. The sudden change in behavior, and its predictable recurrence, meant something had triggered the shift.

But what?

Ghosts usually had a reason for everything they did. Unfinished business, unresolved trauma, or even an emotional connection to a specific time of year. If Vera was throwing a seasonal tantrum, then something about Christmas—or maybe winter itself—had to be a factor. Maybe it had been the anniversary of her death, or the date of some event that had left her unsettled in the afterlife.

Ashlyn frowned, running a hand through her hair as she mulled it over. Perhaps it was something that happened at the Bed and Breakfast itself?

She'd seen it before—an unintentional stirring by guests, renovations, or even emotional energy from living people passing through. Could someone staying at Lilac Grove have unknowingly sparked something? A guest with ties to Vera's past? Or maybe a family tradition that reminded Vera of something she'd lost?

Ashlyn crossed her arms, staring at the holiday lights outside. It wasn't just the usual haunting that interested her—it was the transformation itself. Harmless pranks turning into fire-starting rages. It was too much like other cases, ones that hadn't ended well. A ghost that suddenly gets violent is often a ghost that's about to unravel.

"Whatever it is, I'll find out soon enough," she muttered, feeling the hum of anticipation that came before every case.

She snapped her laptop shut, her mind buzzing with half-formed theories. Crossing the room to her closet, she pulled out a stack of sweaters. New Hampshire in December demanded layers, and she wasn't about to face restless spirits without some cozy knits.

As she tossed sweaters, jeans, and wool socks onto the bed, a sudden chill brushed past her. She didn't even flinch.

"Hello, Hank," she said, reaching for her duffel bag. "Decided to pop in, did you?"

The air shifted near her, tingling with the presence of her old friend. Hank had been hanging around since she'd first moved in. He wasn't much for conversation, just a presence she found comforting—like a lazy cat who liked to watch her pack. He'd never said why he stayed, and she'd stopped asking years ago.

"Going somewhere cold," she added, folding a sweater. "Got a spirit need of some ghost therapy."

The curtain by the window fluttered, though the window was closed. Hank's version of a sarcastic eyebrow raise. She smiled. "I know. Nothing says 'happy holidays' like an angry spirit lighting things on fire."

Ashlyn grinned as she tucked a bundle of sage into the corner of her bag, followed by a pendulum and a few crystals. Some people would roll their eyes at her "essentials," but she'd found they worked just as well as any high-tech gadget. Still, she tossed in an EMF meter and a digital recorder. She liked to balance the mystical with the tech-savvy—it was part of her charm.

As she continued packing, her eye caught a holiday card on the table from Ella Hawthorne—one of her clients with a hint of the gift, someone she kept in touch with. The cheery scene of snowmen and carolers reminded her of how distant she was from most people. She spent her life reuniting spirits with unfinished business, yet she hadn't worked hard on her own relationships.

Her thoughts wandered back to her parents. They'd been gone for so long now. Then she sighed and shook her head, forcing herself to focus on the task at hand. Dwelling on the past wouldn't pack her bag. She zipped up the last compartment and glanced around the room to make sure she hadn't forgotten anything.

Then she crossed the room and set the alarm on her phone for an early morning start. It would be an easy drive, only a few hours assuming she beat the snowstorm, but the sooner she got there, the better. Something about Vera's unpredictable holiday behavior had her on edge.

She tossed the phone onto her nightstand, feeling Hank's presence nearby.

"Well, Hank, I guess this is it," she said, turning toward the window where the air seemed to shimmer, the subtle sign that he was listening. "Off to another haunt. Try not to get bored while I'm gone, alright?"

The curtain stirred, despite the fact that the window was shut tight.

She padded over to the window, her breath fogging the glass as she gazed out at the scene below. Snow coated the streets in a perfect holiday postcard way—lights twinkling along rooftops, wreaths hanging on doors. The warmth of it all felt far away, like a scene she could see but never quite touch.

"Merry Christmas to me," she whispered, her voice tinged with irony. Spending the holidays with a moody ghost, a bed-and-breakfast in danger, and whatever secrets the past was about to dig up? Typical.

But even with the loneliness pressing in at the edges, there was a tiny flicker of excitement in it all. Something new. Something interesting. She didn't mind the ghosts—they were more reliable than most living people. But there was still a part of her, buried deep, that hoped maybe this time, she'd learn something she didn't expect. Maybe Vera's unfinished business would bring answers she hadn't even known she needed.

Ashlyn glanced once more at the snow-covered street before climbing into bed. "Goodnight, Hank."

A faint rustling at the curtain was his only reply.

With that, she pulled the blankets up to her chin. Tomorrow, the road to New Hampshire would unfold before her, and with it, whatever mysteries awaited at Lilac Grove.

CHAPTER TWO

O Come, All Ye Restless

The drive to Laconia was uneventful. Ashlyn had beaten the storm, though the news had made it sound like the blizzard of the century was about to descend. Instead, snowflakes drifted from the sky as she pulled up to the inn, a soft blanket already forming on the ground.

A weathered sign by the road read "Lilac Grove B&B," with a long driveway leading to a grand Victorian home that loomed ahead. The house stood like something out of time, its peaked roof and intricate trim framed against the snow. Delores had decorated the place with simple, tasteful lights—warm, golden twinkles along the edges of the porch and roofline. It was beautiful, like driving straight into a Thomas Kinkade painting.

Ashlyn questioned the point of decorating just for her. Electricity wasn't cheap, and no one could see the lights from the road. But who was she to question what brought someone else joy? If hanging lights made Delores happy, that was reason enough. Ashlyn had learned long ago that small acts of beauty—no matter how unnecessary they seemed—had their own value.

As she stepped out of the car, the crisp air biting at her cheeks, Delores and John were already making their way down the steps of the front porch to greet her. They looked like the quintessential New England couple, bundled in flannel-lined jackets and practical boots. Delores was sturdy and soft all at once, her graying hair pulled back in a neat bun, while John had the quiet, weathered face of someone used to hard winters and long hours.

"You must be Ashlyn Alden!" Delores called, her voice warm and bright, matching the glow of the house. Without hesitation, she wrapped Ashlyn in a hug. "I'm a hugger. I hope you don't mind."

It wasn't the polite, surface-level embrace Ashlyn often tolerated from strangers. Delores hugged like she meant it, her sincerity radiating from the moment her arms wrapped around Ashlyn. For a second, Ashlyn froze, not because she didn't like the contact, but because it was so *genuine*. She could sense when people were faking, their emotions layered with awkwardness or obligation. But this wasn't that. Delores was the real deal, and her warmth eased some of the tension Ashlyn didn't realize she'd been carrying.

John, standing a few feet back, extended his hand in a more restrained but friendly greeting. "Good to meet you," he said, his voice a quiet rumble.

Ashlyn smiled, taking his hand in hers. "Likewise." His handshake was firm but gentle, a perfect complement to Delores' exuberance.

As she stepped back and took in the couple before her, Ashlyn felt a surprising sense of ease. She didn't meet people like this often—people who were exactly what they appeared to be, no pretense, no hidden agendas. Delores and John weren't trying to impress anyone; they cared. About their inn, about the spirits in it, and about the people who passed through. It was clear in their smiles, in the way they stood close together, and in the simple joy they took in greeting her.

Ashlyn loved them already. They were good people—solid, grounded, and real. People you could trust to look out for you, whether you were alive or a wandering spirit.

With all its beauty, the place evoked a strange, sorrowful energy that Ashlyn couldn't quite put her finger on. It certainly didn't come from the Millers—those two were practically made of sunshine and warm cookies. No, this was something else. Something darker. It felt like frustration, like the house itself was holding its breath, ready to burst with whatever it was keeping bottled up.

It made her feel uneasy, though not afraid. Could it be Vera? Perhaps.

"We're so glad you're here!" Delores said, beaming, as John hefted Ashlyn's suitcase up the stairs. They made their way inside to a grand entryway that was, frankly, ridiculous in the best possible way. A Christmas tree dominated the space, soaring at least twenty feet into the air, covered in ornaments that looked like they'd been chosen with great care. There were delicate glass birds, twinkling lights, and ribbons that spiraled down the tree like soft whispers of snow.

"Did you do all this?" Ashlyn asked, impressed. The place could have graced a magazine cover.

"Oh, I picked out the decorations," Delores admitted with a modest wave of her hand, "but John did the lights and the heavy lifting. I get dizzy just thinking about ladders."

John gave a shy smile, a man proud of his handiwork and even more clearly still head-over-heels for his wife.

"Well, it's gorgeous," Ashlyn said with a grin. "Way more than I need."

"Nonsense, honey! You just take care of our Vera," Delores said, her voice warm as fresh-baked pie.

They moved into the heart of the house, and Ashlyn took in the grand tour. The place was a textbook Victorian, all elegance and charm, but with the cozy touches that made it feel like a home rather than a museum. The kitchen was a sprawling affair with wooden cabinets, gleaming copper pots hanging above the island, and the faint smell of something sweet, like cinnamon and apples, lingering in the air.

They passed a library that had Ashlyn slowing her pace, drawn to the towering shelves crammed with old, leather-bound books and a pair of wingback chairs just begging for someone to curl up in them with a cup of tea. A sitting room off to the side boasted heavy drapes, deep armchairs, and a piano in the corner.

"All the bedrooms are upstairs," Delores continued, leading the way up a creaky but solid staircase. "There's also a back stairwell down to the kitchen if you feel like sneaking a midnight snack."

They reached the landing, where the hallway branched out to reveal four doors on either side. "We've got four double rooms, four king-and-queen rooms, and one suite." Delores shot Ashlyn a wink. "Naturally, we're putting you in the suite."

Ashlyn couldn't help but smile as they reached her door. Each room had a small plaque outside with a name engraved on it. "The Lilac Suite," hers read. The others were named after local flora and fauna.

"Small touches make a house a home," Delores said, noticing Ashlyn's gaze.

Ashlyn stepped into her room, where everything from the quilt on the bed to the faint scent of lavender in the air made her feel both welcomed and on edge. That same uneasy energy lingered, tucked just under the surface.

"I'm sure she wants to get settled in, dear," John said, cutting through Delores' well-meaning chatter with the gentle authority that only comes with years of practice.

"Oh, yes, of course." Delores straightened the already perfect bedspread, her hands smoothing out non-existent wrinkles. "I left some lunch meat, cheese, and bread in the kitchen if you'd like to make yourself a sandwich. And I'll bring muffins and breakfast things in the morning.

Tonight, we'd love to have you over for dinner, if you're willing. I've got a lasagna all ready to pop in the oven. We can tell you more about Vera, and—"

"Let's give her some peace, dear," John interrupted again, his voice as calm as ever.

"Oh, yes, of course." Delores flashed a quick, apologetic smile. "Ah! I do the shopping on Mondays, so just give me a list of anything you need, and I'll make sure you're all stocked up."

John took her hand and guided her toward the door, his touch full of affection rather than urgency. "We're just down the drive, about a quarter mile. Follow the path along the lake, and you'll find us. Dinner's at six."

"Thank you," Ashlyn said, touched by their warmth. She already liked them both—Delores with her constant bustling, so eager to make everything just right, and John, the quiet, stoic counterbalance. He radiated calm, a deep-rooted steadiness that seemed to ground Delores in the best way. Ashlyn could see what a good team they were. Where Delores fussed, John reassured. Where she flitted, he steadied.

As the door clicked shut behind them, the room fell into a comfortable silence. Ashlyn exhaled, feeling the tension she hadn't realized she was holding unwind. She wandered over to the window, pushing aside the lace curtain to peer out. From her view, she could see the lake shimmering through the trees, a glint of silver against the deep green of the pines.

She shivered, though the room wasn't cold. That unsettled feeling still lingered, a whisper of something just out of reach. Not malevolent—just *watchful*.

"Vera," she murmured to herself. Whoever Vera was, her presence was in every corner of this place, from the creak of the floorboards to the shadows that stretched long in the afternoon light.

With a sigh, Ashlyn turned back to the room, noting again the little touches that made the Lilac Suite feel both cozy and—well, if she was honest — eerie.

She shook off the thought and headed downstairs to make herself that sandwich. Maybe a little food would help ease the tension. Besides, a house this big deserved to be explored, and she wasn't about to miss out on what had to be an over-the-top Victorian kitchen.

As she passed the sitting room, something flickered in the corner of her vision. She stopped. Turned. A woman was sitting in the rocking chair near the window, swaying back and forth, the wood creaking in the quiet room. Ashlyn's heart jumped in her chest, but not with surprise. It was almost a relief. She'd expected a haunting, and there it was, like a guest who'd arrived a little early to the party.

The woman in the chair wasn't a shadow or a mist or some vague impression of a person. No, this ghost was as solid as if she'd walked in off the street. She was dressed in an old-fashioned gown; her graying hair pulled up in a tight bun, the kind of look that said she wouldn't stand for any nonsense. She narrowed her eyes at Ashlyn like a strict schoolmarm. Then she tutted, a soft, disapproving cluck, shaking her head before fading away as quickly as she'd appeared.

Ashlyn sighed. One might think that seeing a ghost would inspire terror or at least mild alarm, but she'd been dealing with spirits for so long that it barely registered as more than a curious inconvenience. Still, she wasn't expecting *this* ghost to pop up so soon. Usually, the house took a few days before throwing its spectral residents at her.

"I'm just here as a guest," Ashlyn said aloud to the now-empty room, her tone light but respectful. If Vera—or whoever the rocking-chair woman had been—was nearby, it was best to start things off on the right foot. "My name's Ashlyn Alden. Pleased to make your acquaintance. I hope we can be friends."

The room remained silent, but Ashlyn could feel the air shift, as if someone was contemplating her words.

With a small shrug, she turned back toward the kitchen. The smell of cedar lingered in the hallway, mixing with something floral that hadn't been there before. Whether it was Vera's perfume or just the house, she couldn't say.

The kitchen, when she reached it, was enormous. It sprawled out with long counters, a farmhouse sink that could double as a small boat, and an island that looked like it could seat half a dozen people. Copper pots hung from hooks above the island, gleaming in the soft light, and a collection of mason jars lined the shelves, filled with spices and dried herbs. There was a comforting warmth in the space, the kind that made you want to stay and bake something from scratch, even if you did not know what you were doing.

Ashlyn made herself a simple sandwich and ate standing at the counter. The uneasy energy from before had settled into something calmer, though she could still sense that watchful presence lingering in the background. If Vera—or whatever spirits lived here—wanted to talk, they could take their time. She wasn't in a rush.

After finishing her meal, Ashlyn wandered back through the house, finally making her way to the library. It was the coziest room she'd seen yet, with bookshelves that stretched up to the ceiling, filled with all manner of old, well-loved volumes. A small fireplace sat in the corner, and she couldn't resist lighting it. The flames crackled to life, casting a warm glow over the room.

Settling into one of the deep, overstuffed chairs, Ashlyn pulled a book off the nearest shelf—something old and musty, perfect for a quiet winter's afternoon.

As she flipped through the pages, the tension in her shoulders eased. The house might be haunted, but it was also lovely. A perfect spot for the holiday season.

Later that evening, Ashlyn bundled up in her down coat, knit hat, and scarf, taking the path along the lake to the Millers' house. The driveway wound around too, but it seemed ridiculous to drive such a short distance—even if it was freezing. And it *was* freezing. A cold that sinks into your bones and makes every breath sharp, your lungs tight with the crisp bite of winter air. As she stepped onto the path, the snow crunched underfoot, that squeaky sound that only comes when it's dry and packed hard by the chill.

The lake, dark and still, stretched out beside her, a smooth pane of ice that mirrored the twilight sky. Occasionally, the wind skimmed across it, whistling through the bare branches of the trees, and she swore she could feel it trying to sneak under her scarf. Her cheeks prickled with cold, and her gloved fingers were already numbing. She picked up the pace, her breath coming in little clouds that disappeared into the night.

When she reached the Millers' house, a small red manufactured home that stood out against the snow, she sighed with relief. Simple, comfortable, and welcoming. It was a house that didn't try too hard to impress, but made you feel you'd just come home from a long day. She knocked, and as soon as the door opened, a wave of warmth washed over her. It wasn't just the heat—it was the smell. The savory aroma of lasagna hit her like a soft punch to the stomach, and it growled in response.

John greeted her with his usual quiet smile, stepping aside so she could step into the glow of the house. The door opened into the dining room, and Ashlyn couldn't help but notice the table was already set.

"Let me take your coat, dear," Delores said, bustling over to help Ashlyn out of her winter layers. She could feel her face thawing, the prickling sensation of blood returning to her fingertips.

Once her coat and scarf were whisked away, Ashlyn settled at the table. The food was delicious. The lasagna was rich and cheesy, perfectly seasoned, and the homemade garlic bread had just the right amount of crunch. As they ate, Ashlyn shared stories about some of her past cases, ghosts she had met, and the work she did with spirits. To her relief, the Millers weren't put off by it at all—in fact, they seemed interested. John listened with quiet attention while Delores peppered her with questions. By far, they were some of the easiest people she'd ever worked with.

Over dinner, the conversation drifted to Vera.

"So, when did you realize Vera was going to be a permanent guest?" Ashlyn asked.

Delores exchanged a glance with John. "Well, we first saw her in the garden, of course—just standing there, clear as day. But after that, she started making herself known in... smaller ways. Little things around the house."

John nodded, leaning back in his chair.

"It started with the flowers in the parlor," Delores continued. "We'd just brought in a new bouquet, and I'd arranged them in this vase on the mantel. Thought they looked quite nice, honestly. But Vera? Well, she didn't agree."

Ashlyn raised an eyebrow. "Oh? How could you tell?"

Delores chuckled. "We went out for groceries that afternoon—gone for maybe an hour or so—and when we came back, the entire arrangement had been scattered, The flowers were everywhere. It was like she was saying, 'No, no, this won't do at all.'"

John added, "I just looked at them and said, 'Guess Vera doesn't like your taste.'"

Delores swatted him with her napkin. "He acted like it was the most normal thing in the world! Me? I nearly jumped out of my skin." She shook her head, a smile still playing on her lips. "But that wasn't the end. Next morning, I found the candlesticks on the mantle had been rearranged. Moved just a few inches over, but it was clear—she had her own ideas about where things belonged."

Ashlyn grinned. "Sounds like she's got a knack for interior design."

Delores laughed. "That's one way to put it. And it wasn't just the parlor. Over the weeks, little things started happening all over the house—picture frames tilted, curtains pulled back just so. It took me a while to realize it wasn't random at all. She's got an eye for detail, our Vera."

"She definitely prefers things her way," John added. "Once we started calling her by name, things calmed down a bit. I think she appreciated the respect."

"Does that mean you did some research?"

"We did," Delores replied. "She seemed to be dressed in late 1800s clothing, so we dug around in the house records and town archives. Turns out, the house once belonged to a couple named Vera and Andrew Beaumont. When Andrew passed, Vera stayed on for a few years, but we couldn't find much about her after that. No solid death record, no mention of whether she moved away or died here."

"She seemed pleased when we started using her name, so we think we got it right." John said.

"The moment we called her Vera, the house just felt ... lighter. Like she'd finally gotten what she wanted. No more rearranging the furniture or turning the pictures upside down—well, not as often, anyway."

John chuckled, "I think she still likes to remind us who's in charge now and then."

"Sounds like you've found a way to live in harmony with her," Ashlyn said, smiling. "A bit of give and take."

"Exactly. We treat her like a part of the family." Delores said. "I leave out fresh flowers for her sometimes, and in return, she lets us be. It's her home as much as it is ours."

There was a brief pause as Ashlyn absorbed that. The way the Millers spoke about Vera wasn't just with the detached curiosity of people living in a haunted house—they spoke about her with genuine warmth, like she was a quirky but beloved relative.

"Do you ever feel like she's trying to communicate anything?" Ashlyn asked after a moment. "Beyond just rearranging the décor?"

John thought for a second, then said, "I think she wants the house kept in good order. It was hers, and she loved it. As long as we look after it, she looks after us."

Ashlyn smiled. "It sounds like you've built a good relationship with her."

"Mostly," John replied.

Delores sighed, glancing at John before folding her hands in her lap. "The reason you are here…" she said. "Things change around this time of year."

Ashlyn's brow furrowed. "Cany you give me more details?"

Delores glanced toward the window, where the moon had slipped behind a veil of clouds. "Something about the season stirs her up. We noticed it the first year we stayed open through the holidays. Vera gets… more active. And not in a good way."

John's expression hardened. "It starts small. Lights flickering, doors refusing to stay shut—or refusing to open. But as the month progresses, it's like there's this pressure. She gets restless, sometimes angry."

"What does she do?"

Delores answered. "One year, we had a guest locked in her room. The door wouldn't budge. John had to force it open, and when he did, the windows were frosted over—on the inside."

"And another time," John added, "the Christmas tree tipped over in the middle of the night. I'd put it up myself, and it was solid. But it came down, smashed half the ornaments, and scared the guests half to death."

"And the fire..." Delores started, but did not continue.

Ashlyn shivered. "Has anyone been hurt?"

"Not yet," John said. "But it's like she doesn't know her own strength during the holidays. She becomes... unpredictable."

Ashlyn leaned forward, using her most comforting voice. "This is exactly what I'm here for. You don't need to worry. I've handled spirits that react to anniversaries, holidays, even certain scents. It's always tied to something unresolved. If Vera's growing restless around Christmas, there's a reason behind it. We just have to figure out what it is, and help her deal with it."

Delores relaxed a little. "We've tried asking her, but she never answers. At least, not in any way we can understand."

"It sounds like it could be tied to a memory. Something about Christmas has a deeper significance for her—possibly something painful." Ashlyn pondered out loud. "I'm confident we can figure this out."

Delores gave a small smile. "Just don't get hurt, dear. She doesn't mean to lash out."

"I understand," Ashlyn said. "But this is my job. I'm here to help Vera, and I won't let things get out of hand."

The room fell into a thoughtful silence. Ashlyn could feel their concerns. She broke the silence with a practical tone, steering the conversation back to her task. "If I want to dig into Vera's past, where's the best place to start?"

John, grateful for the shift, answered. "The public library on Main Street. They've got records going back to when the town was founded. That's where we found her name in the property records. And there's a cemetery nearby—though we never found a death record for her. Still, it might be worth checking again."

Delores perked up. "And the historical society. They've got old photographs, documents—if Vera was active in the community, there could be something there. I've been meaning to go myself, but—" she trailed off, looking almost sheepish. "I've been a little too afraid to dig deeper."

Ashlyn gave her a smile. "That's what I'm here for. I'll see what I can uncover."

"Thank you. I know it's a lot, and I—well, we—really appreciate you coming to help."

John stood, beginning to gather the plates from the table. "We're lucky to have you here."

The night wound down with warm conversation and the comforting weight of a good meal. By the time Ashlyn made her way back to her room, exhaustion had settled deep in her bones. When she reached the door to the Lilac

Suite, she was more than ready to collapse into bed and let sleep claim her.

But as soon as she stepped inside, she froze.

Her suitcase lay open in the middle of the floor, its contents flung in every direction. Clothes, books, her journal—everything had been tossed about like someone, or something, had rifled through it in a frenzy. Even her toothbrush was lying on the bed, far from where she had left it.

A chill that had nothing to do with the cold crept up her spine.

"Thanks for the welcome, Vera," she muttered under her breath, forcing a wry smile. This was one way to unpack.

CHAPTER THREE

Silent Fright

3 AM. The witching hour.

Some people say it's just a phrase, a bit of folklore to describe the stage of sleep where your body's deep in REM—heart rate slow, temperature dropped, breathing uneven. But there's another theory. One that says when you wake in that dark stretch of night, it's because something woke you.

Ashlyn's eyes snapped open.

At first, she thought she should be relieved. There were no eerie footsteps, no ghostly whispers, no clang of unseen hands tossing pots around in the kitchen. No, this quiet wasn't peaceful. It was too thick, too *intentional*.

Fear crawled up her spine, slow and ice-cold. She wasn't the type to scare easily, but this—this was different. Her heart beat out of sync with the silence, faster and faster, until it pounded so loudly in her chest she was sure something would hear it. She tried to sit up, tried to move, but her limbs refused to obey. Her body was frozen, stiff.

The families she'd lived with as a child had always brushed these moments off as "night terrors." But Ashlyn knew better. This wasn't a dream.

Panic tightened its grip. She tried to scream, to shout for help, but her voice was as paralyzed as her body. Nothing. Not a sound. Not even a gasp.

It felt like hours trapped in that void of silence, with her pulse the only evidence that she was still alive. And then, just as suddenly as it had seized her, the paralysis shattered. The invisible weight lifted, leaving her trembling, her breath shaky and ragged as she pushed herself upright.

She swung her legs off the bed, the cool floor grounding her as she moved to the window. Outside, a fresh layer of snow blanketed the earth.

The clouds had scattered, leaving a bright, full moon hanging in the sky, its silver light so bright it almost looked like dawn.

Ashlyn exhaled, letting the tension bleed out of her muscles. But even as she stared at the serene, moonlit snow, a part of her couldn't shake the feeling that something had just left. Something she couldn't see—but that had been watching her, waiting for that exact moment of stillness.

She turned to crawl back into bed, but something flickered in the corner of her eye.

Her breath caught. There, in the large, overstuffed chair that sat against the far wall, was the woman from the sitting room.

Ashlyn's heart thudded in her chest. The woman sat still, her back straight as a ruler, hands folded in her lap. Her hair, a pale gray that bordered on silver, was pulled into a severe bun at the nape of her neck, not a strand out of place. The high collar of her gown—a somber, old-fashioned thing in deep, dusty black—brushed her jawline, emphasizing the rigid Victorian propriety etched into every line of her posture. Her face was pale, almost translucent in the moonlight, with deep-set eyes that seemed too sharp for the world she no longer inhabited.

Those eyes, hollow but alert, locked onto Ashlyn, studying her in silence.

"Vera?" Ashlyn whispered, her voice only a breath.

The woman didn't move. Didn't blink. Just *watched*, like she was waiting for something.

Ashlyn swallowed, trying to steady her nerves. "I'm Ashlyn," she said, introducing herself to the woman who may or may not even know she was sitting there. The ghost didn't move, just kept watching her with those sharp, glassy eyes.

Her gift had always been unpredictable. Most of the time, hearing ghosts felt like trying to tune into a weak radio signal. The voices faded in and out like distant whispers on a breeze. She could pick up fragments, stray thoughts that slipped through the veil between worlds.

Every once in a while, when a spirit wanted to make itself known, the connection became crystal clear. In those moments, she could hear them as plainly as if they were standing right beside her, flesh and bone, speaking directly into her ear. These were like her childhood friends. The ones that were easier to say were imaginary. Clear as day to Ashlyn.

They could have full conversations, the kind that made her forget they weren't alive anymore.

Most ghosts had their own minds, their own unfinished business, and they didn't always choose to speak. Some didn't even know they could.

Ashlyn waited for that clarity, but Vera's face darkened, her features twisting into an angry scowl. Her sharp gaze, still focused on Ashlyn, seemed to flicker, as if she wasn't seeing her at all.

"You!" Vera spat, her voice trembling. But it wasn't directed at Ashlyn. "Annie! What are you doing in here?"

Vera's expression grew harsher, her back rigid with indignation.

"This is *my* room," she hissed, her voice rising with an old authority that brooked no argument. "You belong in the servants' quarters! Don't think you can just waltz in here and do as you please!"

Ashlyn could almost feel the shift in the room.

"And you've been in here before, haven't you?" Vera's face twisted. "Rifling through my things, stealing what doesn't belong to you. I'll see you punished for this, Annie. Mark my words."

Then Vera blinked, her expression softening as if the fog in her mind had lifted, and for the first time, she seemed to truly *see* Ashlyn standing there. The anger melted into something confused, almost fragile.

"Where... where am I?" Vera asked, her voice wavering. She looked around the room as if seeing it for the first time.

Ashlyn stepped forward, her tone gentle. "You're in your home. My name is Ashlyn." She paused, giving Vera a moment to orient herself. "I'm here to help."

Vera's eyes darted to the window, then back to Ashlyn, wide and lost. "Ashlyn..." she repeated, the name unfamiliar on her lips. "Where is Andrew?" she asked. "He promised... He promised he would be back. Why hasn't he come back yet?"

Ashlyn's heart clenched. She opened her mouth to speak, but before she could find the words, Vera's figure blurred around the edges, like a painting smeared by an invisible hand. Her form grew faint, the lines of her once-sharp face dissolving into the dim light of the room.

Ashlyn let out a shaky breath, her pulse still racing. There was no way she could go back to bed—not after that. The air in the room felt too thick, too charged. Sleep would have to wait.

Ashlyn threw on her robe and grabbed her notebook, her mind restless. The encounter with Vera had rattled her more than she cared to admit, and there was no way she'd find any peace until she figured out what Vera wanted. She headed down to the library and start drafting a plan, something that might give her a sense of control over the chaos swirling around the house.

As she stepped into the kitchen to brew a pot of coffee, her breath hitched. For a split second, she thought she was seeing Vera again, sitting there like a shadow from another time, hunched over in the moonlit glow. But it wasn't Vera.

It was Delores—standing in the middle of the kitchen, dressed only in a robe and slippers, looking dazed.

"Delores!" Ashlyn exclaimed, her voice half-caught be-tween surprise and concern. "What are you doing here? It's not even 4 AM!"

Delores blinked at her, eyes cloudy with confusion. She didn't seem to recognize where she was—or who Ashlyn was, for that matter. Then she sighed, a deep, weary sigh that seemed to collapse her entire frame. "Oh, my... I've done it again, haven't I?" Her voice was soft, filled with embarrassment. "I must have been sleepwalking."

Ashlyn frowned, her heart sinking a little. Delores looked so small, standing there in her thin robe, shivering in the kitchen light. "It's freezing out, and you're in a robe and slippers. Does John know where you are?"

"I'm... I'm not sure," Delores murmured, her cheeks flushing pink. "I didn't mean to—"

"It's alright," Ashlyn interrupted. "Let's get you warm, and I'll call him."

Even though the house was already heated, Ashlyn stoked the fire in the library. The flames crackled to life in the hearth as she grabbed a large woolen blanket from one of the upstairs rooms. She wrapped it around Delores, who seemed more subdued than usual, the faint tremor in her hands betraying her embarrassment.

With Delores settled, Ashlyn picked up the phone and dialed John. She winced as his groggy voice answered on the third ring. "I'm so sorry to wake you, John. Delores is here. She seems to have been sleepwalking."

There was a beat of silence on the other end, followed by a heavy sigh. "I'll be right over," John said, his voice full of concern.

Ashlyn hung up the phone and glanced over at Delores, who was gazing into the fire. Her eyes were distant, as if the flames might reveal an answer she couldn't quite grasp. She shifted in her chair, pulling the blanket tighter around her shoulders, as though it could shield her from more than just the chill.

After a long stretch of quiet, Delores spoke, her voice barely more than a whisper. "Things have been a bit... off lately."

Ashlyn tilted her head, staying quiet, letting Delores take her time.

"I haven't been sleeping right," Delores continued. "Not just tonight. It's been happening more and more. John... well, I think he's worried, but I've been brushing it off. You know me." She gave a weak chuckle, but there was no humor in it. "I keep telling myself it's nothing, that it's just a phase. Maybe stress. But I keep waking up in strange places... like tonight."

Ashlyn's heart tightened at the vulnerability in her voice. She leaned forward, resting her elbows on her knees.

"Delores, it's okay to be scared," she breathed. "But if things feel off, it's worth talking to someone. A doctor could help—maybe it's something small, something fixable. It doesn't have to be scary."

Delores looked at her, her eyes watery in the firelight, the flickering flames casting long shadows over her face. "I've been meaning to make an appointment," she admitted, her fingers twisting the edges of the blanket. "But... what if it's not something small? What if it's... something I can't come back from?"

Ashlyn reached out. "You don't have to face it alone. You've got John, and I'm here now. No matter what, knowing is better than wondering. You're stronger than you think."

Delores let out a breath she seemed to have been holding. "You're right. I know you're right. It's just... terrifying."

Ashlyn gave her hand a gentle squeeze. "I get it. But sometimes, facing the unknown is less terrifying than letting it live in your head. And if you need someone to go with you, I'm here."

Before Delores could respond, a knock echoed through the room.

"John doesn't need to knock to get into his own house," Ashlyn said with a smile.

"He's always been so polite. I sure love that about him."

Ashlyn made her way to the entrance and opened the door to find John standing there with a smile of relief.

"She's fine, and cozy in the library," Ashlyn reassured, stepping aside to let him in. "Just a little cold and a bit embarrassed. But we've got her warmed up now."

When they got to the library, John's eyes found Delores. "You gave me quite a scare, love," he said, his voice low but tender.

"I'm sorry, John," Delores whispered, "I didn't mean to."

"You never do," John replied, walking over to her and draping an arm around her shoulders.

Ashlyn gave them a soft smile, though uncertainty nagged at the back of her mind. She wasn't sure what was going on. The sleepwalking, the confusion—it felt like more than just a rough night. Still, she didn't want to jump to conclusions. All she knew was that a warm fire, and a blanket didn't seem like enough to fix whatever this was.

"It's early," Ashlyn said, eyeing the clock. "But since you're both here, how about some breakfast? I've got bread and cheese, and I think I saw a few eggs in the fridge."

"That would be lovely," Delores replied, her voice still a little shaky from the morning's events.

Delores attempted to help with breakfast, but Ashlyn waved her off with a grin. "You just relax and let me handle this."

They shared a simple breakfast of toast and eggs. The quiet clatter of forks against plates seemed to fill the silence, making the house feel almost normal again. Almost.

"So, I met Vera," Ashlyn said, breaking the stillness.

Delores glanced up. "I know it's only been one night, but... Vera's been quieter since you arrived. Maybe you're having a good effect on her."

Ashlyn paused, then shared the story of the suitcase and the eerie 3 AM incident. As she finished, John leaned forward, looking thoughtful.

"That's why you knew Dolly was here," he said, nodding as if a puzzle piece had just clicked into place.

"It's been quiet this last hour, though," Ashlyn started, but the words barely left her mouth when a loud crash echoed from upstairs.

"I might've spoken too soon!" she said, standing up just as the temperature in the room plummeted. Doors began slamming upstairs, one after another, in a rapid, rhythmic sequence that felt anything but random.

Ashlyn grinned, but her smile was more a mask for her alertness than amusement. "Let me go see what's going on."

At first, it seemed like Vera was having fun. A gust of wind swept through the house, even though the windows were all tightly shut. Holiday decorations fluttered—Christmas baubles rolled off the tree, lights flickered, and the wreath twisted until it was hanging upside down. Ashlyn watched the spectacle, feeling Vera's presence. There was a mischievous energy to it, like a child testing boundaries.

Ashlyn caught sight of Vera's faint, flickering form near the tree. Silver bulbs clustered at the bottom, a lone red one dangled from a branch that couldn't hold its weight, and garlands were draped haphazardly across the tree like a child had gotten into the decorations and called it art.

"I think the star goes on top, Vera," Ashlyn called out, trying to be funny.

Vera paused, her head tilting, as if considering the suggestion. Then, with a grin, she flung a string of lights across the room, letting them sail through the air before they tangled themselves around a lamp. Ashlyn couldn't help but wince. *Okay, then.*

For a moment, the whole thing almost felt lighthearted, like Vera was just having a bit of fun, but as soon as Ashlyn relaxed, the surrounding air shifted.

Ashlyn took a deep breath, knowing this was the part where things could spiral if she wasn't careful. "I think you and I should talk," she said, keeping her voice steady but firm. "I know this is your home, and I respect that. But it's not just you here anymore. There has to be some compromise. Why are you angry?"

Vera's form solidified, her face twisting in a sort of amused disdain. "Angry?" she quipped. "Who says I'm angry?"

Ashlyn raised an eyebrow, glancing at the tangle of lights now draped over the couch. "Well, normal people don't throw lights around..."

From the doorway, John and Delores were watching, their expressions hovering somewhere between confusion and fascination. Ashlyn felt awkward. She was standing in the middle of their house, talking to someone only *she* could see, and they were witnessing the entire thing. *Great first impression.*

"Is she there?" John asked, his voice a little hesitant, like he wasn't sure if he really wanted to know the answer.

"Yep," Ashlyn replied, her tone a little too casual, given the circumstances. She shot them a quick smile, hoping they weren't regretting having her around. *I wonder what they think of me now,* she thought, picturing their conversation once she left. Something like, *'You remember that time we invited a psychic to stay, and she started chatting with our Christmas tree?'*

Vera, meanwhile, hovered by the tree, watching the exchange with mild amusement, as if she found Ashlyn's attempts at negotiating entertaining. The tension in the air remained, though, and Ashlyn knew she had to keep the situation from tipping into something worse.

"Look, Vera," Ashlyn said, turning back to the ghost. "I'm not here to make things harder for you. But we need to figure out how to live together. So, are we going to have a conversation about this, or are you just going to keep redecorating?"

Vera let out a small, almost mischievous laugh. "We'll see," she said, her form flickering as she hovered near the ornaments. Then she was gone.

Ashlyn let out a breath she hadn't realized she was holding. "Well, that could've gone worse," she muttered.

"Did it... work?" Delores asked from the doorway.

Ashlyn shrugged, eyeing the now-untangled string of lights. "She's thinking about it."

"This was a bad idea," Delores said, her voice shaky, her hands twisting together. She looked distraught, her eyes filled with concern that seemed to weigh her down. "You're such a sweet girl. What if Vera hurts you?"

Ashlyn forced a reassuring smile, even as her stomach knotted. "It's okay," she said, the words feeling sharper than she meant them to. "This is what I do—everything's going to be alright."

I hope I'm telling the truth. The thought whispered in the back of her mind, and she shoved it down. Delores was already teetering on the edge of worry, and the last thing Ashlyn needed was for her to see how rattled she felt. She could handle this. It wasn't her first haunted house, after all—but something about this place, about Vera, gnawed at her in a way she couldn't quite shake. Still, she had to keep her calm, if only for their sake.

Delores stood there looking so tired, fragile even, with John standing next to her, his hand resting on her arm. The older couple seemed out of their depth, and Ashlyn couldn't help but feel a pang of guilt.

"Now," Ashlyn said with a gentle but firm tone, "you go make that doctor's appointment, and I'm going to get down to work."

John and Delores exchanged a glance and gave her a reluctant smile. As they headed toward the door, John turned back and offered a kind but weary grin. "Remember, you're always welcome at our place, anytime you need a break from... well, the ghost."

Ashlyn smiled back, grateful for the offer, even though she had no intention of leaving Vera unsupervised. "Thank you. I'll keep that in mind."

Then, almost as an afterthought, she added, "Hey, I've got a colleague who doesn't live too far from here. Is it okay if I reach out to him for help? Maybe let him stay a night or two?"

Sebastian would get a kick out of this, and she'd feel safer knowing she wasn't alone.

John raised an eyebrow and then glanced at Delores, who gave him a playful swat on the arm.

"It's not like that!" Ashlyn blurted, her cheeks flushing. "We're just friends."

John chuckled, and Delores gave her a knowing smile. "Of course, dear," she said, trying not to giggle. "Whatever you need. We trust you."

As the door clicked shut behind them, the house fell into a thick, oppressive silence, leaving Ashlyn alone with her thoughts—and Vera. She stood in the empty kitchen, staring at the last wisps of steam curling from the coffeepot. Her nerves hummed in the quiet, and it felt as if the very walls absorbed Vera's presence.

Ashlyn exhaled, a shaky breath that did little to ease the cold grip of unease settling over her She'd promised Delores that everything would be fine, but the truth was, she didn't have a clue what Vera wanted—or worse, what she might do next.

Spirits could induce fear, sure, but not always out of malice. Sometimes, they just wanted to be left alone, their emotions tangled up with the living in ways that felt like an attack but were more akin to a plea. Yet... was that what this was? Did Vera just want peace, or was there something darker lurking behind those sudden bursts of rage?

There was a certain Jekyll-and-Hyde quality about Vera that Ashlyn couldn't ignore. One moment, she was quiet, almost pitiable in her isolation. The next, she was slamming doors and making her presence impossible to ignore. It made Ashlyn wonder: Was Vera angry because she was trapped here—or because she had no intention of leaving?

A loud thud echoed from upstairs, the sound that made your heart skip a beat even though you weren't sure why. It was followed by deliberate, heavy footsteps.

Ashlyn froze, her pulse quickening. Her body wanted to stay put, but she forced herself to move, turning toward the stairs even as her stomach twisted.

"Well," she muttered under her breath, her voice thin in the quiet, "here we go."

With a deep breath, Ashlyn placed one foot on the first step. The wood groaned beneath her, the creak unnervingly loud. She hesitated, listening. The footsteps above her stopped, too—pausing as if whatever was up there was waiting.

Her hand gripped the banister so tightly her knuckles ached, as though the thin rail could somehow protect her. Maybe Vera wasn't done with her redecorating spree. Or maybe—Vera was done with her.

Ashlyn's skin prickled as she took another step. The temperature seemed to plummet, the cold not just seeping in but clawing at her bones, biting in a way that wasn't playful this time. It felt angry. Dangerous.

Something was watching her.

Waiting.

"Please don't push me down the stairs," she whispered, as if saying it any louder would provoke the very thing she feared. Spirits could be unpredictable, their moods mercurial, especially when they were cornered. Or scared.

But was Vera scared—or something else?

"We don't want to banish you," Ashlyn said, her voice shaky as she tried to reassure Vera.

The whisper came, like an icy gust curling down the staircase, low and venomous.

"You won't take me alive..."

Ashlyn's breath caught in her throat. Her heart pounded, and for a moment, she stood frozen, her blood running cold. This wasn't just a restless spirit trying to make its presence known. This was fury. Real, unfiltered fury.

A door creaked open above her. The sound was slow and deliberate, as if to punctuate the ghost's words. A warning.

Ashlyn had promised Delores that everything would be alright. She had said it with a confidence that now felt naïve. As she stood there, on the brink of something far darker than she'd expected, she could only hope she'd be able to keep that promise.

CHAPTER FOUR

Have Yourself a Scary Little Christmas

Ashlyn's pulse hammered in her ears as she stared up the staircase. *Was that in the Lilac suite?* The door above had stopped creaking, leaving the house in silence.

You won't take me alive...

Her mind latched onto the whisper, puzzling over it. *What does that even mean?* The fear she'd felt in the moment had already evaporated, like morning mist under a rising sun. Dealing with Vera was like riding a rollercoaster: all fun and games on the climb, but just when you thought things might be safe, your stomach dropped, and suddenly everything was chaos.

She swallowed, her throat dry as dust. *Water. I should start carrying a water bottle. Wouldn't that make me look professional—* "Ashlyn Alden, ghost whisperer and hydration enthusiast." An icy breeze snaked down the stairs, lifting the hair on the back of her neck, as if someone—or something—was brushing by.

And then it was gone.

Ashlyn froze. *Wait... what?* Had Vera fled? Some spirits were shy—skittish things that hid in dark corners, or wanted to be left alone. But not Vera. No, her antics practically *begged* for attention. Most of the ghosts Ashlyn delt with either clung to their space like territorial barn cats or threw temper tantrums loud enough to rattle windows. But this... this was something else entirely. *Vera didn't seem like the type to just disappear.*

The whisper now replayed in her mind, softer this time. Less like a threat, more like a plea, shot through with raw, exhausted desperation.

Okay... so, what scares a ghost?

If Vera was worried about being taken, that begged two questions: where had she run to? And, more importantly—*what* was she running from?

Ashlyn's stomach tightened, and before she could think twice, she hurried up the stairs. "Vera? Vera, are you still here?" she called, her voice echoing into the stillness.

The hallway stretched out before her, with doorways leading into shadows. She peeked into one room, then another, half-expecting Vera to pop out, arms folded, wearing a scowl and ready to chastise her for being nosy.

Nothing.

"Where the hell did you go?" Ashlyn muttered, rubbing the back of her neck.

This was feeling less like an investigation and more like a round of hide-and-seek. *Not exactly my specialty...*

She moved from room to room, her boots making soft, deliberate thuds on the worn floorboards. "Vera, come on," she called, exasperation creeping into her voice. "I'm not here to hurt you... unless you're planning on the whole pushing-me-down-the-stairs thing again, in which case, I'd *really* like to renegotiate."

Still no response.

The house had been buzzing with Vera's presence earlier—now, it just felt... *abandoned.*

Ashlyn paused at the top of the stairs, chewing her lip. What was she missing? Her thoughts drifted back to what the Millers had told her. Their first encounter with Vera hadn't been in the house.

It had been in the garden.

Ashlyn groaned. *Of course. The garden. Why wouldn't the ghost hang out somewhere freezing and miserable?* The dead didn't care about seasonal blooms—or frostbite.

She gave the house one last look before heading toward the stairs. *Okay, garden it is. Vera, you better be out there. Because if I freeze to death searching for you, I swear I will come back and haunt you.*

She bundled up, pulling on her coat and scarf, the wool scratching at her neck as she braced herself for the bite of the chilly December afternoon.

The air outside was biting at her cheeks and coming out in small puffs as she stepped onto the porch. She followed the narrow path around the house. It was lined with stone that peeked through patches of snow and made its way toward what must have been a stunning garden in the warmer months.

Now, bare lilac bushes stood like skeletons along the edge of the garden beds, their branches tangled against the pale winter sky. Even in the winter, Ashlyn could almost smell the soft, heady sweetness of their blossoms, the memory of it lingering in the cold air.

To her left, a trellis stood, woven with the dormant tendrils of a climbing vine—honeysuckle, maybe. In the spring, she imagined it would be alive with tiny flowers, their sweet scent drawing bees and butterflies. For now, the vines were stiff, clinging to the wooden structure, refusing to let go and waiting for warmer days to return.

There was a strange stillness here. It was beautiful, yes, even in its barren state, but it felt... watched.

She pulled her coat tighter and followed the path deeper into the garden. The snow crunched beneath her boots, each step echoing in the otherwise quiet air.

"Vera?" she called out. "I know you're here. Or, at least, you've been here before."

The wind stirred, rattling the dry branches of the lilac bushes, but there was no answer.

As Ashlyn rounded the corner, she saw it—a small alcove nestled between two bare lilac bushes, sheltered by a trellis that looked like it might once have held a cascade of flowers. Two stone benches flanked the space, their surfaces frosted over. And there, on one of them, sat Vera, arms wrapped around herself like she was trying to hold her form together.

Ashlyn approached with caution, her footsteps slow and deliberate.

Vera's eyes lifted to meet hers, filled with a quiet, aching sadness that made Ashlyn's heart squeeze in her chest. The woman's form, once an angry, swirling mist of rage and grief, was now opaque. No longer the vengeful, flickering figure from before. Ashlyn could feel it—Vera had shifted.

The fury had drained out of her like the last traces of a storm, leaving only a heavy, hollow silence in its wake.

Ashlyn hesitated, the cold gnawing at her fingers and biting at her nose, but she didn't turn away. "Vera?" she whispered, softer than she meant.

The ghost didn't move. She just sat there, her expression distant and lost.

Ashlyn slowly lowered herself onto the opposite bench, the stone so cold it seemed to seep right through her coat. "Hi," she said gently. "Do you remember me? I'm Ashlyn."

Vera blinked, her gaze flickering back to her, as if she had to reassemble herself piece by piece from wherever her thoughts had drifted. "Yes," Vera answered, her voice thin. She glanced around, as though expecting someone to appear from the shadows. "Where is Andrew? He was supposed to come back."

Ashlyn had learned not to lie to the spirits. It never went well. But there was such a raw, hopeless edge to Vera's voice, she didn't want to crush it. Bits and pieces of the past were spilling out now, offering Ashlyn a place to start.

"I don't know," she said, gently. "But I'll find out."

Vera looked so fragile, as if the slightest breeze might blow her away.

"Where did Andrew go?" Ashlyn asked, keeping her voice steady.

"I..." Vera's face clouded, her brow knitting together as if she were sifting through a long-buried thought. "I don't remember. But he promised to be back by Christmas." Her voice wavered. "He left Annie to take care of me."

"Annie?" Ashlyn repeated, filing the name away for later.

"My nurse," Vera said, her tone shifting to something softer, almost nostalgic. "And our serving girl. She was my helper."

Helper. That explained a lot. Vera must have been ill. The pieces of her story were falling into place, though there were still plenty of jagged edges left to fit together.

Ashlyn opened her mouth to ask another question, but the change came fast—too fast. Vera's expression twisted, going sharp and bitter like a sudden frost. The warmth drained from her voice as she shot to her feet with a startling abruptness, sending the frost-laden branches around her shivering in protest.

"She stole my money," Vera hissed, her voice low and venomous. "I *know* it."

And just like that, she was gone—vanishing into the shadows as if carried off by the wind, leaving only the faint rattle of dead leaves in her wake.

Ashlyn let out a slow breath, feeling the sudden stillness settle over the garden again. "Well," she muttered, brushing a stray lock of hair from her face. "That's a start."

She replayed Vera's words in her mind, sorting through what she knew so far. *Vera and Andrew Beaumont.* The Millers had confirmed that much. Andrew had gone away at some point, and Annie—the nurse, or perhaps a servant—had been left to care for Vera in his absence.

It was a promising lead. Household records might mention Annie, and if Ashlyn could track those down, she'd have something solid to work with. But this case was already shaping up to be more complicated than she'd expected, and Vera's erratic nature was becoming... concerning. This wasn't the kind of ghost she wanted to handle on her own—and the last thing she needed was to drag the Millers any deeper into it.

No. She needed backup. And she knew just the person for the job.

Sebastian LaRue.

Another medium, though *medium,* didn't quite capture the full extent of Sebastian's energy. Where Ashlyn preferred to keep her abilities discreet, Sebastian was about as subtle as a neon sign in the dead of night. Flashy, dramatic, occasionally ridiculous—and absolutely effective.

Beneath all the theater, the man had genuine talent. And, more importantly, he *loved* what he did.

Ashlyn could already hear his voice in her head: *"Honey, spirits want attention, and I am here to give it to them."* She could see the exaggerated wink, the flair of a brightly patterned scarf, and the playful way he'd strike a pose, as if every conversation was a photoshoot waiting to happen.

His parents had been real flower-power types—free-spirited, metaphysical hippies who'd raised him to embrace the mystical without shame. While Ashlyn had spent her childhood keeping her abilities hidden like a guilty secret, Sebastian had thrown himself into his gift with open arms and unshakable confidence.

Yeah. He'd be perfect for this. And, as a bonus, they'd have some fun along the way.

Ashlyn pulled out her phone, already scrolling through her contacts.

***

Vera stayed unusually quiet for the rest of the day and well into the night. It was as if the haunting had sapped whatever energy she possessed, leaving her no choice but to drift off into some unseen corner to recoup. For once, Ashlyn had the place to herself. She should've felt relieved, but instead, it left her on edge. Quiet ghosts were rarely harmless; they were simply reloading.

By the time Sebastian arrived the next day, the stillness was pressing on Ashlyn's nerves. And, of course, Sebastian's entrance shattered it completely. He swept into the B&B with all the energy of a gale-force wind.

His knock was followed immediately by the door swinging open. He wore a long black coat, and a bright scarlet scarf trailed around his neck like a living thing. A fedora sat at an angle atop his silver hair.

"Darling, it's so good to see you!" Sebastian sang, throwing his arms wide as Ashlyn came to greet him at the door. He pulled her into a warm, exaggerated hug, somehow managing not to wrinkle a single seam of his meticulously tailored coat. "This place! Absolutely charming. So quaint, my dear—how positively adorable."

Ashlyn couldn't help but grin at the way he said "adorable," as though it were both a compliment and an insult.

"Come on, you big show-off," she said, shaking her head fondly. "Let me show you the rooms, and you can pick your favorite. And fair warning—Vera is our resident ghost. She's not shy, so don't be surprised if she introduces herself before dinner."

Sebastian arched one elegant brow, handing her his hat. "Oh, thank you, dear. I've always enjoyed a bit of ghostly company—far better than most living people, wouldn't you say?" He winked.

They climbed the narrow staircase; the wood creaking underfoot, and Ashlyn thought back to the first time she met Sebastian. He'd swept into her life the way he approached everything—dramatic and charming. She'd been young and lost, fumbling her way through the spirit world, and he'd taken her under his wing. Now, she had her own wings. He was a bit of a father figure, though she'd never tell him that.

As they reached the landing, a gust of cold air gusted down the hallway. Sebastian gave an exaggerated shiver. "Ooh, yes. There's something unresolved here," he murmured, eyes narrowing as he scanned the dim hallway. "Vera, you said? She's not just angry—she's confused. I can feel it. There's a lot of pain buried under all that flair."

Ashlyn nodded. It was what she'd been sensing, too—though Sebastian always seemed to put things into words before she could. It was one reason she respected him, despite his antics.

"Come on," she said. "Let's see if you like any of the rooms."

The first stop was the Violet Room, where soft purples and grays wrapped the space in a calm, understated elegance.

"My favorite, aside from my suite," Ashlyn said, opening the door with a gentle creak. The quilt on the bed was hand-stitched, the furniture simple but cozy. "It's peaceful."

Sebastian took one glance inside and let out a snort so exaggerated it bordered on theatrical. "Darling, you know I'm no shy violet." He didn't even bother to step inside, already sashaying down the hall with a flick of his scarf.

Ashlyn shook her head, grinning despite herself. Some things never changed.

Further down the hall, they stopped at two more doors: the Peony Room and the Iris Room. The little brass nameplates gleamed under the soft glow of the hallway sconces.

Sebastian paused, inspecting the nameplates as if weighing the merits of each flower with deadly seriousness.

"The Iris," he murmured. "A showstopper, no doubt—elegant, but bold. Refined, yet a little wild. They command attention. Like a performer wearing silk and feathers. Mmmm, tempting."

He trailed his fingers along the brass plate before turning to the Peony Room.

"But peonies," he continued, "oh, darling, peonies are lush drama queens. Unapologetically dramatic. They're divas—stealing the spotlight wherever they're planted. A peony doesn't just exist; it demands to be adored."

He turned the knob with a flourish; the door creaking open. Inside, the Peony Room was a riot of blush pinks and velvety reds, soft gold accents catching the light. The scent of rosewater drifted faintly from a porcelain dish on the dresser. It was the sort of room that expected admiration.

Sebastian stepped inside, surveyed the space with a satisfied smile, and spun on his heel to face Ashlyn.

"There's no question," he declared. "I am a peony."

Ashlyn leaned against the doorframe, arms crossed. "You realize you just compared yourself to a flower, right?"

Sebastian raised one hand, regal as a monarch granting an audience. "It is not mere comparison, my dear. It's destiny."

Ashlyn laughed, the tension easing from her shoulders. "You are impossible," she said, still chuckling as she turned to leave.

"And you," Sebastian called after her, "need to spend more time with the living. Honestly, Ashlyn, you can't let ghosts be your only social circle."

She glanced over her shoulder. "Why not? They're usually quieter."

Sebastian grinned. "Get ready, darling. I'll unpack, and then you and I are having a night on the town!"

His bright, uninhibited laughter echoed down the hall as she walked away, a sound that warmed the old house. It was good to have him here; she thought—not just for his insight, but for the way he pulled her back to the surface whenever she started drifting too far into the spirit realm.

When they left the B&B, Ashlyn drove toward town, stopping at a gas station to fill up and grab a few flyers from a rack by the door.

"Ooh! Ice skating at Opechee Park!" she squealed, pointing at a poster. "We should do that!"

Sebastian made a face, his nose crinkling as though she'd suggested ice fishing. "Darling, that sounds dreadful. Cold and physical? No, thank you. But," he added with a dramatic sigh, "I'm here for you, honey. Lead on."

While the pump clicked away, Ashlyn stepped up to the counter with a snack and the gas payment. The cashier, a young guy with long stringy hair, glanced up with all the enthusiasm of a bored sloth.

"So," Ashlyn asked, "what's fun to do around here?"

The kid blinked, then shrugged. "Uh... bars. Drinking. That kinda thing." He handed her the change without making eye contact.

Ashlyn gave him a thin-lipped smile. Sebastian had been sober for ten years, and taking him to a bar wasn't happening. She leaned on the counter. "Anything that doesn't involve drinking?"

The cashier blinked again, like the concept had never crossed his mind, then shrugged. "You could go to Funspot."

Ashlyn tilted her head. "Funspot?"

"Oh..." Sebastian drawled, already unimpressed. "That sounds... fun."

Ashlyn snorted, tucking the change into her coat pocket. "Come on, grumpy. First, we're going ice skating. Then we can check out this mysterious Funspot."

Sebastian sighed dramatically, but he followed her back to the car without complaint, scarf trailing like a bright banner of resignation.

They headed out as the afternoon sun cast a golden glow over the snow-covered town. Opechee Park looked like it had been plucked straight from a holiday postcard, with skaters gliding across the frozen cove and the distant sound of holiday music drifting from hidden speakers.

Sebastian, naturally, looked like he'd just stepped off the cover of a winter fashion catalog. His black coat swirled behind him as he adjusted his fedora, bright scarf tucked just so. They rented skates from a grumpy man in a parka, who gave them a suspicious glance.

"This," Sebastian muttered, eyeing the scuffed rental skates, "is going to end badly."

Ashlyn waggled her brows. "Confidence, darling." She said, mocking him. "Confidence and momentum—that's all skating is."

"Momentum is what worries me," he muttered, lacing up his boots.

Once on the ice, Ashlyn took to it with effortless grace, gliding in easy loops like she'd been born skating. Sebatian, on the other hand, looked more like a baby deer encountering ice for the first time. He wobbled, arms pinwheeling as she fought for balance.

"Use your legs!" Ashlyn called.

Sebastian shot her a mock glare. "Helpful advice. Truly."

She barked a laugh, the sound clear and unexpected. Despite the cold air stinging her cheeks, a warmth spread through her chest. Sebastian had a way of making everything seem lighter.

After a few more wobbly laps—and only one near-catastrophic fall—Sebastian finally gave up, shuffling to the edge of the rink and leaning on the wooden railing to catch his breath. Ashlyn glided up beside him, not the least bit winded, a triumphant grin on her face.

"See? This is what you need," he said, nudging her with his elbow. "More skating. Meanwhile, I'll be right here, on the sidelines, where it's safe and sensible."

Ashlyn snorted, her breath puffing in the cold air. "You? Sit on the sidelines? Not a chance."

Sebastian chuckled, adjusting his hat. "I'd make it look good, though." He gave her a sideways glance. "I'm telling you, darling. You've got to find more things like this. With the living."

They took a break at the concession stand by the rink, cupping their hands around steaming mugs of hot cocoa, piled high with whipped cream. Ashlyn sipped hers slowly, letting the warmth chase away the cold that had settled in her bones.

The arcade was a few miles away and a lucky discovery, even if most of the machines were older than Ashlyn. They took turns at an ancient pinball machine with chipped paint and flickering lights. Sebastian was a showoff, dramatically tilting the machine just enough to win without setting off the alarms. Ashlyn's attempts ended with flippers flailing uselessly and her score somewhere in the gutter.

"You are the absolute worst," she told him after he racked up his second high score.

Sebastian grinned. "I prefer to think of it as charmingly competitive. Again?"

He didn't wait for her answer, already plunking another quarter into the slot. The machine sat there, lifeless, as if it had given up on entertaining them.

Sebastian's brow furrowed. He gave the machine a stern look, then kicked it with the heel of his boot. "Give me back my money, you rusting monstrosity!"

A kid standing nearby—couldn't have been more than seventeen—strolled over, hands in the pockets of his oversized hoodie. Without a word, he gave the side of the machine a casual slap, followed by three sharp punches on the opposite panel. With a flicker and a groan, the machine whirred back to life, lights blinking as if it had never stopped working at all.

Sebastian's face lit up, his previous frustration forgotten. "Amazing! You're like the pinball whisperer!"

The kid just shrugged, heading back to another machine.

"Hey!" Sebastian called after him. "Do you work here?"

"Yeah," the boy replied. "I keep these babies running." He gave the pinball machine an affectionate pat, then glanced back at them—really looking this time. His eyes narrowed.

"Wait a minute," he said. "You guys are on that ghost hunting team, aren't you?"

Sebastian, sensing an opportunity, straightened up a little taller, as if sitting on a throne rather than a sticky arcade stool. Ashlyn winced. She'd done a few TV shows with Sebastian—and a few solo projects of her own—but she preferred to slip through crowds unnoticed. Not Sebastian. Sebastian thrived on recognition like a plant in sunlight.

"I am," Sebastian announced with a grin.

The boy's face brightened. "You doing a show around here?"

"Nothing for TV," Ashlyn answered before Sebastian could start making promises. "We're investigating the Lilac Grove B&B."

The kid's expression shifted, his brows lifting. "Nice. That's the place where they tried to take that lady to the asylum, right?"

Ashlyn blinked. That was new. Ghost stories did not come with neat little summaries, and sometimes locals had the missing pieces she didn't even know she needed.

"What do you know about the story?" she asked, trying to sound casual.

"Not much," the boy admitted with a shrug. "My girl-friend's more into that stuff. But I think, way back when they used to lock people up in asylums, they wanted to take this rich lady. She didn't wanna go, though. Put up a fight, from what I hear."

Ashlyn leaned forward. "Did they take her?"

The boy shrugged again, unfazed. "Not sure. Never heard what happened after that."

Ashlyn exchanged a quick glance with Sebastian. This wasn't just another ghost with unfinished business—this was a woman who might have fought tooth and nail against being erased. And now, decades later, that fight had somehow carried over into the spirit world.

Sebastian gave a brief hum, the corner of his mouth twitching in thought. "Well, that complicates things."

Ashlyn nodded, already piecing together what this new thread could mean.

As they walked back to the car, the night air crisp and starlit, Ashlyn realized just how much she'd needed this—a break from ghosts and mysteries, a reminder that life could still hold joy. Sebastian had always known that.

And the truth was, she didn't mind. It was good advice.

CHAPTER FIVE

Oh Haunted Night

Ashlyn had always felt invisible. Like the moment she left a room, everyone forgot she'd ever been there. She wondered if Vera felt the same way—trapped in a house full of people, yet unseen.

It had been that way for as long as she could remember, bouncing from one foster home to the next. Not the worst off—not by a long shot. Some of the other kids had horror stories, living in places that never should've been called homes. She'd been lucky, she supposed. The families she'd stayed with were mostly safe, if not warm. Sure, there were the ones who tried to pray the demons out of her, or worse, trotted her out in front of their friends like some parlor trick. But they didn't mean harm. Compared to what she'd seen others go through, well, that was nothing.

But the loneliness—that had been the hardest part. The way no one seemed to care about the little things, like what her favorite cereal was. Or that she hated mushrooms. None of them ever asked, just as no one had asked why Vera was throwing such violent tantrums around Christmas.

She stopped expecting people to notice after a while. Learned to blend in. Just another fixture in the house until it was time to leave. Always have a bag packed, waiting by the door. She knew she'd be forgotten soon enough. Even here, in Lilac Grove, she hadn't fully unpacked (although Vera had helped by throwing her stuff everywhere.) It just made things easier.

She was grateful; she supposed. Really, she was. But sometimes she wondered what it would feel like if someone remembered her. Maybe that's why she kept doing the psychic shows. As "Ashlyn Alden, Psychic Medium," people at least recognized her. Or, more accurately, they knew her face. It was something.

Sebastian had been the closest thing she had to a friend, always reminding her, "Darling, you need to spend more time with the living." He meant well, but it wasn't that easy. The living were exhausting—judgmental, dismissive, too busy with their own lives to notice her. Ghosts, on the other hand, were honest in their misery. They didn't pretend to care. They didn't smile politely, only to forget her moments later.

That's why she kept going back to the dead, wasn't it? Misery loves company, and Ashlyn had found plenty of it among the dead. In some ways, they were the only ones who saw her—just as she saw them. While the rest of the world forgot she existed, Vera was proof that the forgotten would always find a way to make themselves known.

Still, every time Sebastian suggested mingling with the living, she couldn't help but think, *That's easy for you to say. They all love you.* People and spirits alike were drawn to him. He was the life of every room he entered, while Ashlyn felt more like wallpaper. She had spent her life slipping through the cracks, unseen and overlooked.

Today, Sebastian was back at the B&B, seeing if he could connect with Vera while Ashlyn did some research. She had put in a request with the Lake Winnipesaukee Historical Society and was headed there to meet with someone.

One thing she loved about New England was its history. There was never a shortage of historians eager to share what they knew. They got lost in old stories the way she got lost in the past herself. Most of them didn't care that her research wasn't for academic purposes. *History is history,* right?

Her father had been a history teacher before he passed. Sometimes, when she met with these historians, she liked to imagine him sitting there with them. Would he have been like them if he were still alive? Would he have that same glint in his eyes when he talked about some long-dead general or a historic building?

Maybe, in a way, this was why she did what she did—why she sought the dead, trying to pull their stories from the shadows and bring them into the light. Because, deep down, she wanted to believe that just as she remembered her father, someone—*anyone*—would remember her, too.

The Lake Winnipesaukee Historical Society was housed in a yellow building that looked more like a roadside motel than a museum. It was the kind of place you could drive by a dozen times and never notice, tucked away, content to be forgotten.

Ashlyn bypassed the main entrance and headed for a side door marked Historical Society. It creaked open, revealing a room cluttered with desks, old filing cabinets, and the musty smell of well-aged paper. A man with wild, white hair and wire-rimmed glasses looked up from a sea of documents and smiled.

"You must be Ashlyn Alden. My one o'clock," he said, standing up and offering a firm handshake.

"That's me," she replied, smiling back as she shook his hand.

"Glad you're here," he said, waving her toward a chair across from his paper-strewn desk. "Digging into these old records is always fun for me, but sharing what I find? That's the best part. Let's dive in."

Ashlyn settled into the chair as he shuffled through stacks of paper.

"I'm Henry Erickson, by the way—though most folks just call me Hank," he said. "Now, about Vera and Andrew Beaumont. Fascinating couple."

Ashlyn leaned in, eager to hear what he'd uncovered.

"Vera was born in 1827, Andrew in 1822. They married in 1868—late in life, especially for the time. Vera was already in her forties. No children."

Ashlyn's mind raced ahead. "Why do you think that is?"

"Well," Hank said, leaning back in his chair, "Vera inherited quite a fortune when her parents passed away in her early twenties. Back then, if she'd married younger, all of it would've gone straight to her husband, as was the custom. Could be she didn't want to hand over control of her money." He chuckled. "Just speculation, of course, but it seems like Vera wasn't too keen on playing by society's rules."

Ashlyn smiled at that. She liked Vera more and more. "And what about Andrew?"

"Dr. Beaumont," Hank began, pulling out another sheet, "was a well-respected physician. He had strong ties to the New Hampshire State Hospital in Concord. In fact, both Andrew and Vera made a substantial donation to help start their nursing school."

"Tell me about the nursing school." She said.

"It was one of the first of its kind," Hank continued, "established in 1888 with free tuition, room, and board for students. The idea was revolutionary for the time—trained nurses instead of untrained caretakers. The Beaumonts funded part of it. But then their lives took a tragic turn."

Ashlyn leaned in, sensing the shift. "What happened?"

Hank's face turned solemn as he pulled out a faded newspaper clipping. "Andrew died in a train accident in December 1892. He was on a southbound train, heading to Concord. It collided head-on with a northbound freight train just above The Weirs."

Ashlyn felt a knot form in her stomach. She could picture it—the screech of brakes, the deafening crash, the metal tearing apart like paper. She'd seen enough death to know that the end could come suddenly, without mercy.

"The wreckage was catastrophic. Both engines were destroyed, and Andrew was one of several passengers killed. His body wasn't found right away—it was trapped in the debris. From the reports, it sounded like chaos. Two trains, head-on, right by the lake."

Ashlyn stared at the clipping, trying to process it. Andrew's violent death made everything about Vera's grief and anger so much clearer. "And Vera?" she asked. "What happened to her after that?"

Hank shuffled through more papers. "Vera died a year later, in 1893. The cause of death was listed as 'atrophy,' which back then meant she simply wasted away—stopped eating, stopped living. Grief can do that to people."

"Atrophy," Ashlyn echoed. "So, she just... gave up."

"That's what it sounds like. She didn't have anyone left—no children, no family. She likely couldn't find a reason to keep going after losing Andrew."

Ashlyn's mind raced, piecing together what she'd learned so far. Andrew's sudden, violent death. Vera's slow decline into nothingness. And then there was the mystery of Annie. Vera had seemed convinced that someone had taken her money, and that they had tried to take her away. "Did you find anything about an 'Annie' in your research?"

Hank frowned, flipping through his notes. "Nothing concrete about that name, but Vera and Andrew had hired help. Perhaps a maid, or even a nurse. She could've had a caretaker toward the end. The records are murky."

Ashlyn sat back, her thoughts swirling. There was more than Andrew's death and Vera's grief. Something else had happened. Vera had thought someone was after her money—someone she trusted. And if the inheritance had stayed with her after Andrew's death, why would she think it was stolen? And who would have tried to take her away?

"What would have happened to Vera after Andrew died?" Ashlyn asked. "Would she have lost her money?"

Hank shook his head. "No, it would have reverted to her. She was still a wealthy woman."

Ashlyn nodded. The money was still there. So why had Vera felt so threatened?

"Would anyone have tried to... take her away?" she asked.

Hank raised an eyebrow. "It's possible, though she would've had the means to afford care at home. But..."

Ashlyn leaned in. "But?"

Hank's expression darkened. "Do you know what the New Hampshire State Hospital was originally called?"

Ashlyn's heart skipped a beat. She knew exactly what it was called. What kind of ghost hunter would she be if she didn't? But she wanted to hear him say it without bias. "No, tell me."

"It was the New Hampshire Asylum for the Insane," he whispered. "Back in the 19th century, the hospital was one of the few places in the state that offered organized care for the mentally ill. But it wasn't... ideal. It started as a compassionate institution, but over time, like many of these asylums, it gained a darker reputation. Treatments were primitive—things like restraints, cold-water immersion, isolation. Those old buildings have seen more misery than most cemeteries."

"And like most asylums of the time, it wasn't a place you wanted to end up. If someone decided Vera was mentally unfit—grieving too hard, perhaps—they could have pushed to have her committed. And in those days, you didn't need much of an excuse to put someone away."

Ashlyn's blood ran cold. The image of Vera alone in that big house, scared and grieving, haunted her. What if Vera hadn't just been afraid of losing her money? What if she'd been afraid of being locked away, her life controlled by someone she didn't trust? Would this Annie have tried to put her away? It made little sense.

"Thank you, Hank," Ashlyn said, "This is more than I expected."

Hank leaned back in his chair. "It's always a pleasure to help someone who appreciates history. If you find anything else in your, uh, investigations,"—his tone danced around the word — "be sure to come back. I'd love to hear about it."

He handed her a thick manila folder. "Here, I made photocopies of all the important stuff for you. Easier to pin to your murder board that way."

"You're a gem." She smiled, though her thoughts were already slipping away, miles down the road toward the B&B. She stepped outside, and the cold air hit her like a slap. Who had Vera been running from?

When Ashlyn arrived back at the B&B, Sebastian was in the sitting room, fanning himself dramatically with a magazine.

"You okay?" she asked, raising an eyebrow.

"Darling, poor Vera needs a therapist," Sebastian replied with a sigh, his voice dripping with mock tragedy. "She's all hot and cold—one moment she's as angry as a hornet, the next she's frightened out of her wits. I swear, the woman could start a weather pattern with her mood swings. I hope you've found something useful."

Ashlyn smiled, her lips twitching at his flair. "I think I've got a lead."

She gave him a quick rundown of Andrew's death and the few details she'd dug up about their past, watching as his expressive eyebrows rose with interest.

"And what about you?" she asked, leaning forward. "Did you get anything out of her?"

"Well," Sebastian began, setting down his imaginary fan and sitting up straighter, "I had just poured myself a nice cup of tea and was getting ready to commune when she appeared, clear as day, and sat right down like we were old friends. Charming, really. She spoke about her husband, Andrew, and her nurse, Annie."

"That tracks," Ashlyn murmured, nodding.

"But when I asked why she's been acting like a banshee, she just... blinked at me, as if I'd asked her to solve a riddle." He shook his head. "She said she hadn't been feeling well, and that Andrew would be back soon to help sort things out. I pressed her on what he was supposed to help with, but she got all confused. Then, just like that—" he snapped his fingers, "—the mood flipped. She demanded to know what I was doing in *her* house, accused me of trying to take her away, and said Andrew wouldn't allow it. The next thing I know, she's throwing books off the shelves at me like they were frisbees."

Ashlyn winced. "Ouch. She's stronger than she looks."

Sebastian fanned himself again, with real gusto this time. "Darling, 'strong' doesn't quite cover it. If I hadn't ducked, I'd be buried under a pile of Dickens right now."

Ashlyn laughed, but her expression sobered. "I think we need to find Andrew."

"Yes," Sebastian agreed, casting a wary glance at the bookshelves. "Before she turns this cozy little place into a ghostly war zone."

Sebastian leaned back in his chair, eyes narrowing. "Andrew... everything seems to come back to him, doesn't it?"

Ashlyn nodded. "Vera's mood swings seem to center on him—whether he's coming back, or supposed to help her. But there's no sign of him."

"So, Andrew died in a train wreck..." Ashlyn glanced over at Sebastian, who was sprawled elegantly on the armchair. "I think it's time to go full-on investigation mode. If we do not find him here, we can check out that scene next."

Sebastian gave a quick nod, his sharp eyes flicking between the papers scattered on the coffee table. "Agreed." He leaned forward, all business now. "Do you have the details on the wreck?"

Ashlyn fumbled through the stack of papers Hank had given her. After a moment of shuffling, she pulled out a copy of the article, smoothing it out on the table between them. "Right here."

The headline stared back at them: *Local Tragedy: Train Derails Near Laconia, Beaumont Estate Mourns Loss.*

Ashlyn swallowed. The article felt too neat. Too tidy. Andrew was supposed to be the answer to Vera's haunting, but somehow... he still felt like a ghost himself.

They didn't rush. Ghosts didn't care what time of day it was, but the house felt different at night—quieter, with fewer distractions. It made focusing easier. The snow outside added an extra hush to the already still evening, muffling every sound until it felt like the world beyond Lilac Grove had disappeared.

Sebastian was lounging in the library, feet kicked up on a footstool as he fiddled with his spirit box, a faint crackle of static filling the room. "I know you hate this thing," he said, glancing at Ashlyn, who was seated nearby, her hands wrapped around a mug of tea.

Ashlyn shrugged. "I don't hate it. I just like hearing what ghosts have to say without the '80s radio station cutting in."

He flashed a grin, waggling the spirit box. "You're just jealous because it's dramatic."

"You're dramatic," she shot back, unable to resist a smirk. She'd already laid out her own equipment—an

EMF meter, pendulum, digital recorder, and a stack of crystals for good measure. She liked having all the bases covered.

Outside the window, snowflakes fell in a slow, steady drift. The entire scene felt almost too peaceful, considering they were about to wander around looking for dead people.

"I think it's time," Ashlyn said after a while, setting down her mug and stretching.

Sebastian hopped up with the enthusiasm of someone who had been waiting to put on a show. "Let's gather our toys and see who's home."

Vera was nearby, even if she wasn't visible. She'd been trailing them for the past hour, silent but curious, as if trying to figure out what they were up to. Ashlyn had felt her presence—just a light tug on the edges of her awareness.

"She's watching us again," Ashlyn murmured.

"Of course she is." Sebastian didn't even glance over his shoulder. "She's probably admiring my scarf." He adjusted the bright scarlet fabric draped around his neck with a flourish. "Good taste, Vera, if I do say so myself."

They started in the Lilac Suite. Ashlyn always liked to begin methodically, moving from room to room with careful steps, like peeling away layers of the house's energy.

Ashlyn stood by the bed, running her hand along the faded quilt. "Do you think this was their bedroom?"

Sebastian was about to respond when a soft voice, clear and disembodied, answered: "Yes."

Both of them froze, and then Sebastian, never one to miss a beat, turned toward the air as if Vera herself had appeared in front of him. "Thank you, darling. Always nice to have confirmation."

If this *was* Vera and Andrew's bedroom, then it made sense why Vera hovered here so often.

They swept the room, moving from corner to corner. No sign of Andrew. Vera followed them, flitting from spot to spot, watching with a sort of detached curiosity, as if the investigation was a show and she was waiting for the big reveal.

They moved on to the kitchen. Sebastian, ever dramatic, cranked the spirit box a little higher, the static louder now as it scanned the frequencies. The occasional burst of a distant voice broke through—random, disconnected words that meant nothing.

"Well," Ashlyn said, "no signs of anyone else. Just Vera."

It stayed that way as they moved from room to room. The library, with its towering bookshelves and fireplace, felt like it should have held something—some hidden energy. But the only presence was Vera, trailing after them with the quiet persistence of someone waiting for them to figure out something they hadn't quite grasped yet.

"Nothing," Sebastian said, his voice edging toward disappointment as they passed through the sitting room. The rocking chair by the window sat still. Not even a flicker of energy from the EMF meter.

"I'm thinking Andrew's playing hard to get," Sebastian quipped.

It wasn't until they reached the door to the attic that everything changed. Vera, who had been floating nearby like a curious bystander, shifted. Her form solidified, and a sharp chill swept through the air as she moved in front of the door.

Her expression hardened, her eyes narrowing with a fierceness Ashlyn hadn't seen all night.

"It's mine!" she hissed, her voice no longer soft or curious, but sharp, possessive.

Ashlyn felt a prickle of unease at the intensity. "Vera, it's just the attic. We're not taking anything from you."

"She doesn't want us up there." Sebastien stated the obvious.

Vera's figure flickered, her translucent form twisting and distorting as though she were burning through every shred of energy to keep them from opening the attic door.

Then the chaos began.

A door down the hall slammed shut, rattling the walls. Another followed, and then another, as if Vera's rage was shaking the very bones of the house. The lights flickered overhead, dimming and brightening in rapid succession. The spirit box in Sebastian's hand erupted into a burst of static, screeching as if the radio frequencies had come alive, feeding on the raw energy pouring from Vera.

"Vera, stop!" Ashlyn called out. But Vera wasn't listening.

The attic door shook in its frame, rattling violently as if it were going to explode. Every inch of the house seemed to vibrate with Vera's frenzied energy.

And then, just as suddenly as it started, everything stopped. The doors ceased their slamming, the lights steadied, and the spirit box fell silent.

Ashlyn exhaled, the tension in her body refusing to release. "She did this before,. It's like she has to recharge after she throws a fit."

Sebastian gave her a sidelong glance, his hand already reaching for the doorknob. "Well, now that she's taken a little break... shall we?"

Ashlyn grinned. "Naturally."

With Vera's anger still fresh in their minds, they made their way upstairs. The house creaked around them, but

Vera stayed absent. No gust of cold air, no disembodied voice protesting their ascent.

It was unsettling to have her gone, especially now that they were inching toward what seemed like the heart of the mystery.

The attic door creaked open with little resistance, and the dusty air hit them like a wall. Ashlyn half-expected some other spirit to be there—after all, attics were infamous for hauntings—but there was nothing. No lingering ghosts, no flickers of movement in the shadows. Just a stillness that felt more like neglect than a supernatural presence.

The attic stretched out before them, its slanted roof cutting the space into uneven angles. Dusty beams crisscrossed above, and cobwebs hung in the corners like forgotten curtains. Old trunks and furniture covered with white sheets sat haphazardly. In the center, a single window let in a sliver of moonlight, casting pale shadows across the floorboards.

"Attics like this are supposed to be crawling with ghosts," Sebastian muttered, glancing around. "It feels... underwhelming."

Ashlyn nodded, frowning. "Yeah, this is almost disappointing."

They searched the room, moving past piles of moth-eaten drapes and crates filled with who-knew-what. Every corner was checked, but the further they went, the more anticlimactic it felt. No eerie voices, no cold spots. If Vera was hiding something, she wasn't here to stop them from finding it.

It wasn't until they reached the far end of the attic, behind an old armoire, that Ashlyn spotted something. "Sebastian," she called, nudging a crate aside with her foot. There, nestled between the armoire and a stack of old ledgers, was a small metal box.

"Well, well," Sebastian said, crouching down to inspect it. "What do we have here?"

The box was old but solid, its lock covered in a thin layer of grime. Ashlyn knelt beside him, running her hand over the surface. "Looks like it's from the right period. Could this be what Vera was so protective of?"

Sebastian didn't answer right away. He pulled a small lock-picking kit from his pocket—because of course he had one—and got to work. The lock was resistant at first, but within moments, there was a soft click, and the lid popped open with a faint creak.

Inside the box was a single brass key that looked as though it would fit this very lock. It was old-fashioned, with a thick, ornate bow and a long shaft.

Ashlyn picked it up, holding it between her fingers, and tried it without luck. "It doesn't fit this one."

Sebastian's eyebrows arched. "Curious," he said, leaning in to inspect the key. "Why would someone hide a key inside this box?"

Ashlyn frowned, the pieces of the puzzle swirling in her mind. She turned the key over in her hand. "So Vera was worried about her money. But if someone stole it, why was a key left behind? What does it even open?"

Sebastian stood, his usual dramatic flair tempered by genuine curiosity. "That," he said, dusting off his hands, "is what we need to find out. But whatever it is, it's not here."

They had uncovered a clue, but it only raised more questions. What had happened to Vera's money? Did she even have money? Who had taken it? And why had she been so protective of a key that didn't even fit the box it hid in?

Whatever the answer, this mystery was far from over.

CHAPTER SIX

Wreck the Halls

It had been a few days since Ashlyn had touched base with the Millers, though she'd meant to check in sooner. Delores had called the night before, inviting her for coffee in the morning. A nice surprise, though Ashlyn sensed the meeting wasn't entirely casual.

John had been called away to a board meeting—something about Granite State Precision Manufacturing needing his attention—which left just her and Delores. So much for retirement. Despite how in sync the couple seemed, it didn't take a psychic to know Delores had something on her mind.

That suited Ashlyn just fine. Something had been off about Delores that night she'd wandered in half-asleep, and it gnawed at the back of Ashlyn's mind. She hadn't heard how the doctor's visit had gone, and a quiet coffee seemed like the perfect opportunity to check in without pushing too hard.

The past couple of days had been a blur of frustration, with her and Sebastian searching high and low for the box the mysterious key was supposed to open. Despite their best efforts, they'd had no luck. Tonight, the plan was to investigate the train wreck in the hope that Andrew's spirit might finally show himself. Maybe he would have some answers about the key or, at the very least, point them in the right direction. She wasn't holding her breath.

Meanwhile, Vera had been... well, Vera. Running hot and cold, as was her fashion. One moment she'd be calm and almost sweet, the next, she'd be knocking ornaments off the Christmas tree like a disgruntled cat. Sebastian had taken to referring to her as "a doll" when she was in a good mood, followed quickly by, "... when she wants to be." Ashlyn had to agree. There were times when Vera's presence was almost pleasant, like having a stern but protective grandmother hovering nearby. And then there were the tantrums.

They'd both learned the hard way to keep the Christmas lights—and the tree—unplugged. After the third near-miss with a fire, Ashlyn had made it a firm rule.

Vera had a thing about the decorations, and while Ashlyn couldn't fault her for being particular, she also wasn't keen on burning the place down over some tangled tinsel.

This morning, as sunlight peeked through the edges of her curtains, Ashlyn stirred, blinking against the winter glow. The air had that crisp, clean bite that only came with fresh snow, and she could feel the cold radiating from the windows. Outside, the world gleamed, and she winced at the thought of stepping out without sunglasses.

Still, it was a beautiful day, and Ashlyn bundled up, bracing herself against the cold as she made the short walk to the Millers' house. Her boots crunched through the fresh powder, the sound satisfying in the morning quiet. The air smelled sharp and clean, tinged with pine, while the world felt muffled, its usual sounds dulled by the blanket of white covering everything in sight.

"It's so good to see you, sweetie!" Delores greeted Ashlyn at the door with a warm hug, her usual energy a bit dimmer today. "How are things going with Vera?"

"Slow," Ashlyn admitted, stepping inside. "But we've got some great leads."

They moved into the dining room, where the scent of fresh coffee greeted them. It was already set out on the table, steam rising from the mugs in the cool air. It felt welcoming, but something was off. Delores was usually a whirlwind of energy, but today, she seemed more subdued.

"Cream and sugar?" Delores asked, her hand hovering over the tray.

"Just cream, thanks." Ashlyn smiled, trying to lift the mood as she settled into her seat. She recapped their recent discoveries for Delores—how the train wreck had killed Andrew, their investigation of the key, the Beaumont connection to the Asylum, and Vera's atrophy death. Each piece of the puzzle seemed to lead them in a new, darker direction, but Ashlyn was used to that by now.

"Poor woman," Delores sighed, her eyes lingering on her coffee cup like it held answers.

Ashlyn studied her for a moment. "You okay?" she asked. It wasn't like Delores to seem so distant.

Delores took a deep breath. "Just feeling my mortality is all."

There was a long pause, the words hanging between them like the snow outside—cold, inevitable.

"Speaking of that," Ashlyn ventured, "did you ever make it to the doctor?"

Delores hesitated, her expression shifting from embarrassed to something more vulnerable. "I have an appointment today, but I'm thinking of canceling. John got called away, and... I've been feeling much better."

The way Delores' voice lifted at the end made it clear she was trying to convince herself more than anyone else. Ashlyn could see through it—the same way she could sense spirits. She knew when someone was skirting around the truth.

Delores frowned, her honesty breaking through. "John says he thinks I'm fine, but I think we're both just skirting around our fear. What if it's bad news?"

Ashlyn's heart tightened. She understood that fear—how it gnawed at you, made you want to turn away from answers that might hurt. But she also knew how much worse it could be to live in the dark. "What if it's not?" she countered, leaning forward. "What if it's something you can deal with?"

Delores just shrugged, her gaze dropping back to her cup, the uncertainty on her face.

"It's better to know," Ashlyn said. She waited for Delores to meet her eyes. "Tell you what. What if I take you? You shouldn't have to do this alone."

Delores blinked. "You'd do that for me?"

"Of course," Ashlyn replied. "You don't have to face it by yourself."

Delores brightened, a bit of her usual spark returning. "Thank you, sweetie. Really, I don't know what I'd do without you."

Ashlyn gave her a warm smile. "What time's your appointment?"

"11:30," Delores answered.

"Perfect," Ashlyn said, taking a sip of her coffee. "We'll leave from here. It's going to be alright."

Delores drove them to the clinic on Main Street, a small-town medical office shared by several doctors. The place had the usual hum of a busy practice, but the wait wasn't as long as Ashlyn had dreaded. After the nurse took Delores's vitals and asked about her symptoms, they sat together in the quiet exam room.

Delores looked small, folded into herself like a wilted flower, her usual bright energy dimmed by fear. Ashlyn felt a pang of sympathy and filled the silence with something light.

"So," she said, her voice cheerful, "you want to hear about my favorite ghost encounters?"

Delores's eyes brightened. "I suppose I could use the distraction."

"My favorites are the cases where I help not just the people, but the spirits, too," Ashlyn continued, leaning back in her chair. "It's extra special when I reunite lost loves."

"That sounds beautiful." Delores smiled. "What was your last case?"

"Old theater in Boston," Ashlyn said. "Love, murder, mystery—the whole package. And a happy ending, believe it or not!" She winked, earning a soft chuckle from Delores.

Before they could dive into more stories, there was a gentle knock on the door, and the doctor entered. He was an older man, his hair snow-white, with a face that seemed to have been shaped by smiles.

"Dolly! How are we today?" he greeted Delores.

Delores straightened. "Dr. Albee has been treating me since I was in my twenties!" she told Ashlyn, her voice fond.

The doctor extended his hand to Ashlyn, who shook it. "And who might you be?" he asked.

"Ashlyn Alden," she replied.

"She's a friend," Delores added. "John had work, something about the share buyouts, and I didn't want to come alone."

"Still working?" Dr. Albee raised an amused eyebrow. "I thought he was supposed to be retired!"

"I know, right?" Delores chuckled. "He's on the board now—keeps him busy and feeling important."

Dr. Albee gave a knowing nod. "I've seen that happen before." He turned his attention back to Delores. "And how's the B&B these days?"

"Oh, it's marvelous!" Delores beamed. But when her gaze flickered to Ashlyn, she hesitated. "Ashlyn's here, to uh, help us out..." She trailed off, sharing the whole ghost situation. Not everyone believed in spirits, and Ashlyn knew when to keep her mouth shut.

"Well, that's great!" Dr. Albee said, unaware of the unspoken detail. He sat down on the rolling stool and leaned forward. "So, what's going on? What brings you in today?"

"Well, I've been having some memory problems lately," Delores began, her voice wavering. She cleared her throat and continued, "Insomnia. And, um... I've been sleepwalking. When I manage to sleep, that is. I ended up in the B&B the other night, in my robe and slippers."

Dr. Albee frowned. "That must have been frightening for you."

"Thankfully, Ashlyn was there," Delores said. "She called John. He hasn't been sleeping much either because of me."

Ashlyn shifted in her seat, feeling a twinge of discomfort. She didn't know Delores well, but she felt a protective urge toward her. "You don't need to feel bad about that, Delores," she offered. "John loves you. He just wants you to be okay."

Delores nodded, but there was sadness in her eyes that made Ashlyn's heart ache. The woman sitting next to her was so different from the one she'd met only days ago—the one who had shown off the B&B's holiday decorations and talked about lilacs like they were old friends. Now she looked fragile, like her own mind was becoming too much to carry.

Dr. Albee had begun his examination, moving through the usual steps with quiet professionalism. He asked a series of questions, the kind that Ashlyn knew assessed Delores's memory, cognitive function, and overall health.

"Have you had any trouble remembering recent events, Delores?" he asked as he listened to her heart, his tone calm and reassuring.

"Sometimes," she admitted. "I'll forget where I put something or what I was going to do next. But isn't that normal?" She forced a nervous laugh. "I mean, I'm not as young as I used to be."

Ashlyn's mind wandered as Delores answered more questions. She was starting to wonder if Vera might have had similar issues. The way she lashed out, her sudden mood swings, and her erratic behavior... could it be that Vera had been suffering from dementia when she was alive? Could that explain her confusion, her anger? Ashlyn tucked the thought away for later.

Dr. Albee straightened up, pulling his stool closer to where Delores sat. "Here's my concern," he said. "Your symptoms... they're pointing toward the early stages of dementia. But before we go down that road, I'd like to rule out other things—like a vitamin deficiency or thyroid issues. We will get you a blood draw. We'll also make you an appointment to visit a specialist to get a clearer picture."

He paused, glancing at Ashlyn. "John should really be there for that appointment," he added, with a small apologetic smile. "No offense, Ashlyn."

Delores swallowed hard. "What does this mean, Doctor? Am I... am I going to forget who I am?"

Ashlyn's heart clenched. It was such a raw, terrifying question—one that Ashlyn didn't have an answer to, and one she wished no one ever had to ask.

Dr. Albee leaned forward, his expression gentle but serious. "It's a good thing you came in as soon as you started noticing changes, Delores. If this is dementia, catching it early is important. It gives us time to educate you about treatment options and coping strategies. There are medications that can slow the progression, and we can help you manage the symptoms so that you can maintain your quality of life for as long as possible."

Delores sat for a moment, her hands clasped in her lap. "Why me?" she whispered, her voice trembling. "Could I have done something better?"

Ashlyn felt a pang of helplessness. She wished she had something comforting to say, but what could anyone say in the face of something like this? She reached out and squeezed Delores's hand, hoping the gesture would be enough to let her know she wasn't alone.

"It happens to the best of us," Dr. Albee said. "As we get older, these things can creep up on us. But you're not alone in this, Delores. We're going to work together to figure out what's going on, and you'll have your family—and your friends—to help you along the way."

Delores nodded, though Ashlyn could see the unshed tears glistening in her eyes. She wanted to ask more, but she didn't know how to push without making things worse.

Then Ashlyn asked, "Doctor, can dementia... sometimes make people... angry? Like, confused about where they are and... lash out at others?"

Dr. Albee looked at her with a curious expression, his eyebrows raising. "It can," he replied. "In the early stages, some people do experience mood swings, agitation, or even aggression. They might get confused about their surroundings or misinterpret situations. Has Dolly shown these symptoms?"

"Oh no," Ashlyn answered and hesitated before continuing. She couldn't very well explain that she was wondering if a ghost might have had dementia. "I've just... seen it before," she said vaguely. "Someone close to me."

Dr. Albee nodded, satisfied with the explanation. "Yes, it's not uncommon. But again, we don't know for sure what's going on yet. Let's focus on getting Delores the tests she needs and take it one step at a time."

Ashlyn forced a smile, but inside, her brain was spinning. If Vera had dementia when she died... if that confusion and anger had carried over into death... what would it take to help her find peace? And what did that mean for Delores, if she was starting down a similar path? The ride home was silent. Delores looked lost in her own personal hell, and Ashlyn could only imagine the whirlwind of thoughts running through her mind. The woman looked like she was trying to hold the world together with sheer willpower, and it was unraveling right in front of her.

When they arrived at the bed-and-breakfast, they entered together. Ashlyn braced herself the moment they stepped inside.

The sitting room was a disaster zone.

It looked like Vera had hosted a brawl with the Christmas decorations. The tree was half-toppled, lights strewn across the room like discarded party streamers. Broken ornaments littered the floor, glinting in the afternoon light like shards of misplaced hope. Dirt from an overturned poinsettia plant was scattered across the rug, mingling with torn garlands, and picture frames—once hanging neatly on the walls—now lay shattered in a heap. It was as if the room itself had given up.

Sebastian sat in the middle of the chaos, looking absolutely done. He had a rag in one hand and a dustpan in the other. His normally impeccable appearance was disheveled—hair tousled and his scarf askew.

"Darling, I am a wreck," he declared dramatically, as if he were the one suffering the most. "Our lovely Vera was on the warpath again. First, she accused Annie of stealing her money, then Andrew, and—brace yourself—she even blamed you, sweetie," he said, looking at Ashlyn with wide eyes.

Then, spotting Delores, Sebastian shot up from the floor, smoothing his hair and offering his hand. "Oh, my stars, I'm so sorry. Sebastian LaRue, charmed to meet you."

Delores blinked, as though only now registering the world around her. She didn't take his hand. Her gaze swept over the chaos, and her face crumpled.

"Oh my..." Her voice broke as she sighed. "This... this is bad."

Without another word, she made a beeline to the small closet in the corner and retrieved a broom. Her hands shook as she started sweeping up the shattered frames, the delicate glass crunching under the bristles. She moved mechanically, as if cleaning would somehow fix it all—the mess, the haunting, the fear that was building inside her.

Ashlyn watched her heart sinking. The dam was breaking. Delores crouched to gather the dirt from the destroyed poinsettia, tears welling in her eyes, her breath coming out in short, jagged bursts.

"It's too much," she whispered, her voice trembling. "It's all too much!"

Sebastian, sensing the breakdown, stepped in. "Darling," he said softly, prying the broom from her hands with a gentle tug. "Let us take care of this. Ashlyn, please, make this poor woman some tea before she keels over."

Ashlyn nodded, ushering the shell-shocked Delores into the kitchen, her arm a steady presence at her back.

Once they were alone, Ashlyn guided her into a chair, boiling water for the tea. "Has it ever been this bad before?" she asked.

Delores had her head in her hands, her fingers trembling. "It's not just this," she whispered, her voice barely holding together. "It's... it's me. I'll never be able to keep up with this place if I have... D..." She choked on the word, unable to finish. "Dementia," her eyes filled with a raw, quiet terror. "We never should have bought this place. What was I thinking?"

"Honey, we don't know anything for sure yet. Don't give up so fast," she said, keeping her tone light. "Seb and I are going to help Vera, and worst-case scenario, you hire someone to help you keep up with the inn. You don't have to do it all alone."

Delores didn't answer. Her gaze had drifted to something on the table, her attention caught by a small object.

It was the lockbox. Beside it sat the key.

"Oh, what a beautiful key!" she said as she picked it up. "It's... it's a lilac!" Her fingers traced the delicate engraving, the lilac motif wrapping around the handle.

Ashlyn blinked, looking at the key as if seeing it for the first time. How had she not noticed that before? She picked it up, feeling its cool weight in her palm, the strange pull of something old and unsolved.

"Could this be for something in the garden?" she murmured, turning the key over in her hand. For the first time that day, a spark of hope flickered in the gloom.

"Sebastian!" Ashlyn called, "Come here!"

The kettle was boiling, steam curling up into the kitchen air. She poured three cups of chamomile tea, the soothing scent filling the room as Sebastian joined them at the table.

"Look at this key," she said, sliding a cup toward him. "What do you see?"

Delores handed him the key, now looking more alert, a little embarrassed. The emotional storm from earlier had passed, but there was still a flicker of uncertainty in her eyes.

"I'm so sorry," she gushed, her voice regaining its usual warmth. "I'm not usually like that. As you already know, I'm Delores." She smiled, soft but genuine. "Thank you so much for helping Ashlyn. She's a doll, and so are you."

Sebastian placed a hand on his chest. "Oh, darling, thank you. The pleasure is all mine." He examined the key with a raised brow, turning it over in his fingers. "Hmmm, it is a lovely old key," he said, giving a slight shrug. "Got some strong vibes coming off it."

Ashlyn leaned in, watching his expression. "If I tell you it's a flower, what do you see?"

Sebastian narrowed his eyes, squinting at the key as if it might bloom in his hands. Then his eyes went wide. "Oooooh!"

"What's the big deal?" Delores asked, curiosity sparking in her voice.

"I think you found a clue!" Ashlyn said with a grin. She pointed to the delicate lilac motif etched into the metal. "This would make a perfect garden key."

"But the garden doesn't have any locks," Delores said, tilting her head.

"Not that we know of," Sebastian chimed in, his voice conspiratorial.

"I didn't mention the key this morning," Ashlyn continued, her voice dropping into a hush, "because we got a little distracted. But Seb and I found it up in the attic. It was locked in a strongbox. And trust me—Vera really didn't want us to find it. She's been pretty touchy ever since, which explains today's... um... episode." She gestured toward the chaotic mess in the next room. "I think it's important. Maybe it has something to do with the money she thinks was stolen."

Delores frowned, her forehead creasing. "Do you think her money is in the garden? Like buried treasure?"

Ashlyn laughed. "I doubt we need to start digging through the frozen ground with shovels. But maybe, if we can figure out what this key unlocks, we can help Vera settle down." She paused, thoughtful. "Kind of like how we can't treat a problem until we know what it is. Once there's a diagnosis, there's a way forward—even if it's not a cure."

Sebastian nodded, sipping his tea with a flourish. "Ah, like therapy for spirits. We just need to find the root of her troubles."

Their conversation was interrupted by a knock at the door. A familiar voice called out, "You here, Dolly?"

"In the kitchen!" Delores called back.

John stepped in, his face creased with concern. "I saw your car and thought you might be here..." His gaze shifted to Delores, and his expression softened. "Have you been crying?"

Delores blinked. Reality seemed to crash back over her, and she stood up, smoothing her hands over her clothes. "Let's go home," she said quietly. "We've got some things to talk about."

John looked from her to Ashlyn, his brow furrowed with confusion. "What's going on?" he asked.

Ashlyn waved them off with a reassuring smile. "Don't worry, we'll catch up later. Seb and I are doing an investigation tonight—at the site of the train wreck. We're hoping to find Andrew."

"Train wreck?" John echoed, glancing back at Delores.

"I'll explain everything," Delores said, steering him toward the door. "Let's go."

As they left, Ashlyn's eyes lingered on the key, still resting on the table, a quiet mystery waiting to be unlocked.

CHAPTER SEVEN

We Wish You a Scary Christmas

They had planned their investigation of the train wreck carefully. Tonight was the Cold Moon—the December full moon that lingered longer than others. Ashlyn knew that lunar phases, especially during the changing seasons, often heightened paranormal activity. With the solstice just around the corner, this felt like the perfect night to make a connection.

Sebastian drove, squinting at the dark road ahead. Ashlyn navigated as they wound through a sleepy neighborhood.

"Take the next right on Watson," Ashlyn instructed, glancing at the map on her phone.

He turned, focused on the road ahead.

"Now, another right onto Scenic. Look for house number 215," she added as Sebastian slowed. "Here. Park in front of this one. I've arranged with the owners to let us cut through their backyard. There's a path that leads down to the old tracks by the lake."

The car rolled to a stop in front of a cozy little house. A wreath hung on the front door, and the glow of Christmas lights lined the windows. Ashlyn imagined the family inside fast asleep, probably with visions of sugarplums dancing on their heads. At least the owners were kind enough to let them cut through their yard.

Moonlight bathed the snow in a silvery glow, transforming the world into a quiet, glittering wonderland. As they made their way through the yard, the soft light made their flashlights seem almost unnecessary, though Ashlyn kept hers on—just in case something jumped out from the shadows. With so much paranormal energy in the air, you could never be too careful.

The path was narrow and cold, and their boots crunched through the snow as they navigated around branches that clawed at their sleeves. Ashlyn could feel the familiar excitement bubbling in her chest, even if her toes were losing feeling.

Sebastian, however, was not bubbling. "Are we going to get stuck on these tracks and, I don't know, die horribly? Just checking."

Before Ashlyn could answer, a distant whistle cut through the night air. Low and mournful, it sent a shiver down her spine.

"These tracks are mostly for the scenic line now," she said. "Nothing runs at night."

"Except for the ghost trains," Sebastian muttered.

They reached the tracks, a pair of long, frost-covered lines stretching out under the night sky. Sebastian kept a wide berth from them, eyeing the metal rails like they might spring to life and wrap around his ankles. Ashlyn had to admit, with the cold and the moonlight and that whistle still echoing in her head, she wasn't feeling too confident about the tracks either.

"Let's get across and head for the pier," she said. "We'll set up there."

The pier jutted out over the frozen lake. Every step they took made the wood groan beneath their boots, as if the structure itself was debating how much longer it wanted to hold up. At the end, they set their gear.

The frozen lake stretched out in front of them, and behind them, the faint outline of the woods swallowed the world in shadow. Somewhere out there, over a hundred years ago, a train had derailed on a night like this.

"The passenger car is supposedly still down there," Ashlyn pointed out toward the darkness. "It's a historical scuba spot now."

"Is that even a thing?"

"I don't know," she laughed. "I found it mentioned on a scuba forum while researching. Just trying to lighten the mood."

Sebastian set down a battery-powered lantern and began unpacking their supplies. He pulled out a manila folder and opened it.

"This one's my favorite," he said, smoothing the top sheet. "I love the way the journalist described it: 'So great was the force of the collision that the locomotives were welded together. The forward cars, driven by momentum, leapt over them in a wild game of leapfrog.' The writer should've been a novelist."

"Maybe they were," Ashlyn quipped, smiling at the grim poetry of it.

Sebastian continued reading. "The train derailed, slid down the embankment, and skidded out onto the ice before breaking through and sinking." He paused. "Can you imagine that?"

Ashlyn nodded, her gaze drifting toward the lake; the story playing out in her mind.

Suddenly, the wail of a train whistle sounded again, louder this time. It was followed by the screech of metal grinding against the tracks. Ashlyn's breath caught, and in an instant, she was no longer on the pier but right in the middle of the wreck. The deafening crunch of metal echoed around her as the cars collided. She felt the shock as the train broke through the ice, the freezing water rushing in, pulling everything down.

And then she was back. Ashlyn blinked, meeting Sebastian's eyes. Neither of them said a word—they didn't need to. That was the beauty of another medium for a friend. They both understood. You couldn't rush through fear like this; you just had to ride it out like a wave and hope you didn't drown. Being an empath to the dead wasn't a job for the faint-hearted.

They sat in silence, hands clasped, grounding each other until their breathing slowed and the sharp edges of panic dulled enough for them to think straight.

Finally, Ashlyn broke the quiet, her voice steady. "We're looking for Andrew Beaumont."

The wind answered, a faint whisper in the frozen air. "Vera…"

Sebastian straightened. "He's here," he said, a confident note in his voice. "I can feel it."

Ashlyn could feel it too—Andrew's presence, weak and distant. He was there, but just barely, like a man pounding on a door no one could hear. His fear crashed over her in waves, raw and unfiltered, as if he were still beating against the ice, desperate to escape. Panic rolled off him in suffocating bursts, choking. No more whispers now, just blind, primal terror.

Sebastian already had the recorder out. He recorded the empty air, then played it back. The voice crackled through, thin and desperate. "Help… help… help…" The same plea, looping over and over, trapped in his last moments.

Ashlyn's heart broke. It wasn't just fear—it was hopelessness. He'd been stuck in that same moment for far too long, his mind frozen in the instant everything ended. She reached out with her senses, searching for any other spirits to latch onto, but there was nothing. Andrew was alone in this.

"Andrew," she said, her voice dropping into the soothing tone she reserved for anxious spirits and people alike, "it's okay. You're safe now. You're not trapped in the ice anymore."

The air stilled, just for a second—like the tiniest crack. A pause in the panic. But it didn't hold. The fear snapped back, like a beast that couldn't be caged. It was as if Andrew didn't know how to stop, like he'd been terrified for so long, he'd forgotten how to feel anything else.

"Andrew," she tried again. "We're here to help. But I need you to stop—relax. You're safe. We can't help you if you're still freaking out."

Another pause, longer this time. She could almost feel him listening, like he was hovering on the edge of understanding.

"We're going to get you out of this," she added. "But you've got to calm down. Panic won't break the ice—it'll only make it worse."

Her words settled into the air, like the first warm breath of air after a long, cold winter.

"Hello, Andrew," Ashlyn said. "Try the EVP again. I think he's just finding his feet."

Sebastian nodded and clicked on the recorder. They sat, waiting for any sign of response. When he played it back, Andrew's voice crackled through the static. "Help... Vera..."

Ashlyn tilted her head thoughtfully. "Interesting," she murmured. "He's not asking for help from the ice. He's asking for her."

Her thoughts were cut off by a sudden shift in the air.

"Oh—hello!" Sebastian blurted out, his hand moving to his throat. His voice carried an unfamiliar edge, like someone else was nudging their way through. Ashlyn's eyes widened as she realized what was happening.

Andrew was reaching out—trying to connect.

"That's it, Andrew," Ashlyn encouraged. "You can use Sebastian's voice if you need to. Just... share it."

Sebastian opened himself to the spirit. "I'm here," he whispered. "I'm ready. We can do this together."

There was a brief pause, and then a change.

"I need to get home," Andrew's voice said.

Ashlyn glanced at Sebastian, who gave a quick nod, signaling he was fine—though his eyes were a little wider than usual. Sharing a voice with a ghost was no small feat.

"We can help you get home," Ashlyn said, keeping her tone gentle. "But why does Vera need help?"

"She's..." Andrew paused, like someone trying to remember a dream after waking. "She's unwell. And Christmas is her favorite time. I promised I'd be home for Christmas."

Ashlyn's stomach twisted. Andrew Beaumont didn't realize how much time had passed. She could almost feel his confusion hovering just beneath the surface. If she wasn't careful, she'd lose him to it.

"Andrew," she asked, keeping her voice calm, "do you know where you are?"

Another long pause, then: "The hospital," he said, but the uncertainty was creeping in. "I must be. It's cold, but it's always cold in hospitals, isn't it?"

Ashlyn exchanged a glance with Sebastian, who raised an eyebrow. Spirits often latched onto places that made sense to them—hospitals, old homes, anywhere that could explain their current state of confusion.

"It's not a hospital, Andrew," she said. "It's... a little more complicated than that."

The air rippled. "What do you mean?" His voice was tighter now, bracing for bad news. "I was on my way home. The train was late. Vera—she's waiting for me. I promised I'd be home by Christmas."

Ashlyn took a deep breath, choosing her words. "Andrew, listen to me. That train ride... it was a long time ago. The train... didn't make it. It derailed."

There was a beat of silence. "Derailed?" Andrew's voice was strained now. "No. That's not right. I would've... I'm going home. I promised."

"I know," Ashlyn soothed. "But the accident... it happened over a hundred years ago. You didn't make it home, Andrew. Not in the way you think."

Another long pause, and then Andrew's voice wavered. "But I can't be... I'm not..." His words trailed off as the reality of it sank in. "I'm dead."

"Yes. You died in the train crash, Andrew. But you've been stuck here ever since."

The air turned colder, sharp enough that Ashlyn could feel it cutting through her coat. His presence wavered, a flicker on the edge of panic.

"No," he said, his voice breaking. "No, that can't be right. I promised Vera. I promised I'd come home."

"You didn't let her down," Ashlyn said quickly. "You couldn't have known what would happen. It wasn't your fault."

"She needed me," he whispered, the guilt heavy in every word. "I let her down."

"No, Andrew," Ashlyn said. "She's been waiting for you, but she's not angry. She's just... been lost without you. Just like you've been lost without her."

"I was supposed to protect her," he murmured, more to himself than to them. "I was supposed to come home..."

"And you can still keep your promise," Ashlyn said. "You're not stuck anymore. We're here to help you get home, but you need to let go of this... of the guilt. You did everything you could."

There was a long, aching silence. The cold pressed in on them, deeper and sharper, but Ashlyn felt the change—small, like a breath catching in the wind. Andrew was listening.

"How?" he finally asked, his voice only a thread. "How can I get to Vera?"

Ashlyn gave a smile, even though he couldn't see it. "You just have to let go, Andrew. We'll guide you. You can go where you're meant to be. You don't need to stay at the scene of the crash anymore."

The wind seemed to hold its breath. Ashlyn did the same. For a moment, nothing moved, and then Sebastian's shoulders slumped.

"He's gone," Sebastian whispered, his voice almost as quiet as Andrew's had been.

Ashlyn felt her chest tighten. There was that strange, hollow feeling when a spirit left—like something in the air had lifted, leaving it lighter but a little sadder too. Andrew's presence drifted away like a sigh on the night wind.

"He was a quick learner," Sebastian murmured, rubbing the back of his neck with a grimace. "Most spirits take a lot longer to figure it out."

Ashlyn nodded, her breath fogging in the cold air. "Do you think he'll be back here or at the house?" She stared out over the frozen lake, where the moonlight made the ice gleam like glass. "Or do you think he's crossed over?"

Sebastian frowned, staring into the distance as if he could still sense Andrew somewhere just out of reach. "I don't know. It's like he's retreated into a place we can't reach him. He hasn't passed over yet, but he's not here either."

Ashlyn blew out a long breath, watching it curl into the night before vanishing. "I guess that's all we can do for now." She sighed, then gave a half-hearted shrug. "Let's pack up. It's cold enough out here to freeze my eyelashes off."

Sebastian gave her a tired smile, already reaching for the lantern. "That would be a look."

The drive back to Lilac Grove was quiet, the road ahead winding through the snow-dusted trees like a path into a frozen, forgotten world. Ashlyn was in processing mode, sorting through the puzzle of Vera and Andrew. She loved that Sebastian understood this about her, letting the silence settle between them without feeling the need to fill it.

"Thank you, Seb," she said, breaking the stillness. "For understanding my quiet."

"Far be it from me to interrupt the ghost therapist's thoughts," he replied. "Hmmm, maybe you should add that to your title."

Ashlyn smirked. "I think I'd need a therapy license first."

"Mmhmm." He shot her a sidelong glance. He wasn't wrong, though. There was something about her—whether it was her energy or just how the universe seemed to work—that drew these kindred spirits to her. Or maybe it was the other way around.

Andrew and Vera were no different from many of the cases she'd taken on before. Most of the time, the ghosts were separated for one reason or another: evil entities, confusion, guilt. And more often than not, they just needed to get out of their own way. Unfinished business was the term everyone used, but it went deeper than that. People spent their lives fighting the obstacles of society, but after death? The only thing left holding them back were their own notions of what was important.

Her job was to either clear up their unfinished business—or teach them it didn't matter anymore.

Reuniting lovers was her favorite, though. There was something so satisfying about helping souls find their way back to each other after death. Andrew felt like he needed to protect Vera, and Vera? She just needed her love. There was always the chance Andrew had moved on once they freed him from the ice—but in Ashlyn's experience, that wasn't the case. They would see him again.

She felt a strange kinship with him. Maybe Andrew had gone away to process everything, to find the next logical step. It had to be a shock to realize you'd been dead for over a hundred years. That sort of thing took a minute.

Before she knew it, they were pulling back into the driveway of Lilac Grove. The B&B stood quiet, bathed in the soft glow of moonlight. It was close to 1AM, and the house had that peaceful, sleepy look to it—except for the figure on the porch.

Ashlyn squinted, recognizing Delores standing at the front door. She was fumbling with the handle, her movements clumsy and hurried.

"Is that Delores?" Sebastian asked, leaning forward in his seat.

"Yeah," Ashlyn replied, already unbuckling her seatbelt. "Come on."

They hurried out of the car and up the porch steps, finding Delores muttering to herself. At least this time she was wearing her heavy winter coat, but her hair was mussed as if she'd just woken up—or hadn't really gone to bed at all.

"Delores?" Ashlyn said, trying not to startle her. "What are you doing out here?"

Delores jumped a little, turning to face them. There was a distant, confused look in her eyes, as though she couldn't quite place where she was. "Oh, I need to get the room ready," she said, her voice a bit breathless. "There are guests arriving, and I—I can't seem to find the keys..."

Ashlyn's heart sank. She stepped forward, placing a hand on Delores' arm. "It's okay, Delores. There aren't any guests right now. You don't need to prepare anything."

Delores blinked, her brow furrowing. "No guests? But... I could've sworn I..."

"You're just a little turned around," Ashlyn said, keeping her voice soothing. "Let's get you inside where it's warm, okay?"

Sebastian moved to open the door, and they guided Delores in, the warmth of the house enveloping them as they crossed the threshold. Once inside, Delores seemed to deflate, the confusion giving way to recognition.

"Oh no," she murmured, her shoulders slumping. "I did it again, didn't I?"

Ashlyn exchanged a quick glance with Sebastian. "Let's get you comfortable," she said, helping Delores out of her coat.

Delores gave a tired, self-conscious chuckle, shaking her head. "I keep telling John we should strap me into bed, so I stop wandering around in the middle of the night."

Sebastian gave her a kind smile and Ashlyn stepped into the next room and pulled out her phone, dialing John's number. After a few rings, his groggy voice answered.

"John? It's Ashlyn," she said. "I think you need to come over. Delores is here."

There was a pause on the other end before John sighed, the exhaustion clear in his voice. "I'll be right there."

As she hung up the phone, Ashlyn returned to Delores, who was now sitting in the armchair, looking small and vulnerable. "John's on his way."

Delores nodded, her gaze distant once again. "I'm sorry," she whispered, almost to herself. "I didn't mean to cause any trouble."

Ashlyn gave her shoulder a gentle squeeze. "You're not causing trouble, Delores. We've got you."

Ashlyn made her way into the kitchen, the quiet hum of the house settling around her. There was still a plate of cookies on the counter, the store-bought kind she'd picked up earlier. They looked a little sad in the pale light, but they'd do. As she reached for them, she felt a familiar presence—cool, but not unsettling—hovering near her shoulder.

"Hi, Vera," she said, smiling softly, as if speaking to an old friend.

The spirit's energy was gentle tonight, a far cry from the agitation that had filled the house earlier. Ashlyn felt a wave of gratitude wash over her.

"We found Andrew," she said, glancing over her shoulder. "He's on his way."

Vera's form, barely more than a shimmer, seemed to brighten at the mention of his name. Her outline flickered, as if her essence was responding to the hope. Ashlyn wasn't sure if a spirit's eyes could truly brighten, but something in Vera's energy shifted—lighter, more eager. Ashlyn only hoped she wasn't giving her false hope.

She turned to warm some cocoa, pouring the rich liquid into mugs as the smell of chocolate filled the air. Vera drifted near her, the calm presence swirling like a gentle breeze, watching Ashlyn's every move. It felt... domestic, in a way. As if Vera was waiting for the familiar rhythms of a holiday gathering she used to know. Ashlyn arranged the cookies on a tray, adding the mugs of cocoa.

"You always loved Christmas, didn't you?" she asked, glancing at the ghost.

Vera didn't speak, but her form twirled, as if the very memory of it set her dancing. Ashlyn smiled and carried the tray into the sitting room, Vera floating behind her, swaying as though moved by some invisible melody only she could hear.

"I brought treats," Ashlyn announced with a grin, stepping into the room.

Delores blinked, bleary-eyed, and a little confused, as John entered behind her, having just arrived. "But... it's the middle of the night."

"What better time to celebrate?" Ashlyn replied, handing them both mugs of cocoa. John gave her a tired but grateful smile as he took his seat next to Delores.

Sebastian, who had been sitting by the fire, caught Ashlyn's eye. He, too, could feel it—the atmosphere was different now, charged with something gentle and sacred. He rose and made his way to the piano in the corner of the room. His fingers hovered over the keys for a moment before he played, the notes soft and slow, like a memory unfolding.

The melody was faint at first, but Ashlyn recognized it immediately. Her heart swelled as Sebastian sang in a low, reverent voice.

Silent night, holy night.

All is calm, all is bright.

Ashlyn's voice joined his, the words falling from her lips. Outside, the snow continued to fall, the moon casting a pale glow through the windows. In her mind, she could almost picture that night—the one from so long ago. A mother and child, meeting each other's eyes for the first time in that stillness, in that peace.

Round yon Virgin, Mother and Child.

Holy infant, so tender and mild.

The room seemed to glow with the song, as if the spirit of Christmas itself had settled into the old bed-and-breakfast. Delores and John, sitting side by side, sang as well, their voices soft but full of warmth. Even the air seemed to still in reverence.

Sleep in heavenly peace,

Sleep in heavenly peace.

As the last note lingered in the air, Ashlyn looked up—and there, standing in the doorway, was Andrew.

CHAPTER EIGHT

Grim Tidings We Bring

They had finally gone to bed just after 3 a.m. The Christmas carols soothed Vera enough to settle her, and John had taken Delores home. Tomorrow, she had an appointment for a brain scan, which was scheduled for the afternoon.

Ashlyn hoped they'd get some rest. John had said little after the carols ended, but it didn't take an empath to know he was terrified. His hand trembled when he wrapped Delores' scarf around her shoulders, as though he feared even the most basic task was slipping from his control.

When Ashlyn had pulled him aside in the hallway, his eyes had been dark with fear. He stared at the floor when he whispered, What if I'm not enough? The words felt like a punch. John was a man made of quiet strength and seeing him unravel like this tugged at something deep.

She knew that love, no matter how strong, couldn't always keep you from feeling helpless. In fact, it did quite the opposite. Ashlyn had reassured him—but the words felt hollow. She'd seen that same fear in Andrew. And if love was all that was needed, Vera wouldn't still be here. Love is powerful, but fear can make the road feel long and lonely.

Ashlyn watched them leave, John's hand resting on Delores' back, guiding her through the falling snow. They didn't speak, but there was comfort in the silence. She knew that kind of silence, the kind that came from years of understanding.

But now, alone in the quiet house, her mind started spinning again. That Vera might have suffered from some form of dementia in life had been nagging at her for a while, but now it felt undeniable. Vera wasn't just a restless spirit, she was stuck in her own confusion, trapped in the loops of her fading memories.

And Andrew... His guilt, his connection to the state hospital... It all clicked into place. He hadn't just been Vera's husband. He had been her caretaker. Maybe that's why his spirit lingered, tangled up in the same unresolved guilt and helplessness John was feeling now. If Andrew had worked in what was considered mental health back then, he would've known how terrifying it was to watch someone you love to slip away, and the dark place they may end up.

Ashlyn sighed, rubbing her temples. Spirits didn't get better just because they died. Death didn't erase always unfinished business. It just... froze it. Vera had been lost in her mind before she passed, and now she was stuck in that same fog.

It all started making sense, but her brain felt too tangled to untangle it. She had to bring them together—Vera and Andrew—but how? And what did that even mean? Ashlyn did not know what "finishing" their business would look like.

Her mind wouldn't stop racing, and even though it was late, sleep refused to come. When it finally did, a deep, low chime shattered the silence.

Gong...

Ashlyn blinked awake, her body heavy with exhaustion. Did the house have a grandfather clock? She couldn't remember seeing one.

Gong...

She'd barely drifted off when the noise started again. She growled in frustration, pulling a pillow over her head.

But Vera was there, pacing back and forth. *He's supposed to be here. Where is he?* Ashlyn didn't so much hear the words as she felt them—frantic, fragmented thoughts spilling over in waves.

Gong...

The annual party... our friends... Vera's thoughts raced, tangled up in panic. *He left me.*

Gong...

Ashlyn winced, feeling the sharp edge of Vera's fear cut through her. *How am I going to take care of myself? They're going to take me away... they're going to make me leave!*

Gong...

Ashlyn's heart pounded as Vera's confusion overwhelmed her. *I can pay them off... they won't take me...*

Gong...

It's gone... the money's gone... Annie took it...no—Andrew... Andrew took it... Vera's thoughts spiraled, each more erratic than the last. *I'm all alone...*

The relentless tolling of the clock reverberated through Ashlyn's skull, drowning out her own thoughts. She couldn't think straight. The clock, Vera's voice, the thoughts—they wouldn't stop. It was driving her mad.

The thoughts crashed over her in waves—Vera's panic, her confusion, and that ever-present fear that twisted around Ashlyn's own mind like vines, choking her. She could feel it, so real it was suffocating. *He left me... they're going to take me away.* Ashlyn's breath hitched as her vision blurred. She stumbled, the sensation of waiting, of fear, of abandonment clawed at her chest. *Gone... everything's gone...* Vera's thoughts fragmented, pulling Ashlyn deeper into a fog so thick it was like drowning. And somewhere, beyond that crushing despair, the chime of the clock—counting down...

Gong...

And then it started again. *He's supposed to be here...*

A soft rapping caught Ashlyn's attention, pulling her from the swirling haze of half-dreams and confusion.

What was that? Where was she? Who was she?

The door creaked open, and Sebastian slipped in. Concern softened his usual swagger as he rushed to her side, hands gently gripping her shoulders. The contact grounded her.

"I'm here," he murmured, voice soothing.

Ashlyn inhaled, the haze lifting just enough for her mind to clear.

"I felt it too," Sebastian said, his brow furrowed. "I was worried about you. You are closer to this—closer to Vera—than I am."

A shiver ran through Ashlyn. "That was... a powerful manifestation. It's been a long time since I nearly lost myself like that."

Sebastian nodded, his expression serious. "It was intense. But you're safe now. I'm right here."

For a few moments, they sat in the quiet, the only sound the faint ticking of the clock. Ashlyn stared at the window, where the night outside was still thick, the garden cloaked in darkness.

Finally, she spoke. "It all felt so real. But—it's good. I realized something."

She explained the breakthrough, the understanding of Vera's torment. The confusion, the anger—it wasn't just the frustration of a spirit clinging to the past. Vera had been suffering in life. "Dementia," Ashlyn said. "She was already losing herself when Andrew died. And after that, it only got worse."

Sebastian's eyes darkened. "Oh no. Those turn-of-the-century hospitals..." His voice dripped with disdain. "Horror houses, really. I've seen too much pain in places like that."

"Andrew was involved with one in Concord," Ashlyn continued, her mind piecing it all together. "He was a doctor. I don't think he was an evil man... I think he was trying to protect her. To keep her from being institutionalized."

Sebastian gave a slow nod. "You're probably right."

Ashlyn rubbed her eyes. "What time is it?"

"Just before six," Sebastian answered after glancing at his watch. "We've got a couple hours until sunrise."

"Well, we're up." Ashlyn shrugged. "And I'm definitely not going back to sleep. Want to check out the garden while she's quiet?"

Sebastian's expression lightened. "I'm with you."

As they stood to leave, Ashlyn glanced back at the window, where a faint shimmer of frost clung to the glass. "Christmas had always been a strange season for Ashlyn. For other people, it was full of warmth and family. For her, it was something different—a reminder of the homes she'd passed through, of the brief glimmers of happiness that were always too fleeting.

Vera had loved Christmas too, once. Ashlyn could feel that love, the remnants of it clinging to Vera's spirit like old tinsel. But now, that joy was tangled in grief. The holiday had turned into a cruel ghost of itself, much like Vera had. And Ashlyn? Well, she understood that better than she cared to admit.

"Come on," Sebastian said, nudging her. "Let's go see what the garden has to say."

Ashlyn followed him out, her mind still turning over thoughts of Vera, of loss, and the quiet ache that seemed to haunt both the living and the dead during the holidays.

The moonlight had dimmed, but it was still bright enough for them to make out the shadowy shapes of bushes and trees as they trudged toward the garden. Sebastian had grabbed the lilac key from the table, and Ashlyn stuffed it in the backpack with their usual ghost-hunting gear.

Cold air wrapped around them as they stepped outside, sharp and bracing. The garden stretched out before them, a snowy blanket covering everything, and the moon hung low, painting inky shadows that stretched long as they walked.

An unsettling quiet filled the space between the brittle lilac bushes, which stood like bony fingers reaching for the sky. The stillness was almost too perfect.

"What exactly are we looking for out here? And where do we even start?" Ashlyn asked, frowning as she scanned the bare branches and path winding through the snow.

"It would be helpful if Andrew showed his face," Sebastian replied.

"Speaking of," Ashlyn began, giving him a sidelong glance. "Did you see him last night?"

Sebastian froze mid-step, turning, eyes wide. "What? You saw him and didn't mention it?"

A sheepish grin tugged at Ashlyn's lips. "I was tired! It slipped my mind."

"Slipped your mind?" Sebastian let out a dramatic sigh, hands flaring briefly. "Ashlyn, rookie mistake. You should have told me!"

She blushed, the cold hiding most of her embarrassment. "You're right. I was just caught up in the moment."

Shaking his head with exaggerated disappointment, Sebastian reached into the backpack for a small tape recorder. "Andrew, if you're here, we'd really appreciate a conversation," he said, addressing the empty space around them before pressing record. After a few seconds, he rewound the tape and held it to his ear.

A pause. He frowned. "Nothing. Too quiet, if you ask me."

Ashlyn cast her gaze across the snowy expanse. The lilac bushes, bowed under the weight of snow, seemed almost sad. The feeling tugged at her, pulling her attention toward a small alcove hidden in shadow, where Vera's presence seemed to lurk just out of reach.

"We should probably split up," Ashlyn suggested, her eyes lingering on the alcove. "You look for Andrew, and I'll try to coax Vera back."

Sebastian raised an eyebrow, skepticism written across his face, but eventually shrugged. "Sure, I guess," he said, muttering to himself as he head down a winding path deeper into the garden.

Alone, Ashlyn's thoughts drifted—Christmas always did this to her. She couldn't remember much about holidays with her parents; it was a blur of warmth and vague images, nothing substantial. Foster care Christmases had been bleaker—a reminder she didn't have anyone waiting for her. Vera had loved Christmas once, too. The grand balls, the lights, the joy. Now, it was nothing but a tangled mess of grief and confusion festering in her spirit like an old wound.

The flood of memories hit Ashlyn without warning, so sudden and powerful she couldn't tell where her own thoughts ended and Vera's began. She could feel Vera's joy from those long-ago winters, the grand Christmas parties in the very house behind them—music, laughter, warmth. And Andrew. Oh, the way her heart soared when she danced with him, the way the world had felt whole in those moments. It was too much.

Ashlyn doubled over, clutching her head as the memories threatened to drown her. She was waiting again, just like before. But waiting for what? Why was she in the garden? Andrew was gone, and they were going to send her away—they were going to take her. The fear, the help-lessness, it all surged through her, raw and unbearable.

The snow under Ashlyn's knees might as well have been miles away. She could feel it, sure, but only in that distant, numbed way you feel things when your mind is spiraling into someone else's despair. Vera's emotions were like a heavy fog, dragging her down, making it hard to think clearly.

Then, suddenly, there was Sebastian, and his hand land-ed firmly on her shoulder. "Okay," he said, his tone flat, like he was already over this entire situation. "Splitting up? Terrible idea."

The steadiness of his voice yanked her out of Vera's head long enough to take a shaky breath. Ashlyn nodded, still a bit wobbly from it all, but feeling her own thoughts start to separate from Vera's again. Vera was still there, though, lingering at the back of her mind, fractured and confused.

Sebastian looked around the garden and spoke to the air in the most casual way, like he was inviting Vera over for tea. "Alright, Vera. What are we looking for?"

But there was no answer. Ashlyn could still feel Vera's presence, but it was like trying to hold on to water. Her thoughts were slipping away, barely there.

"She doesn't know," Ashlyn said, her voice unsteady. "She... can't remember."

Sebastian squinted into the dark, scanning the area again. His eyes landed on something—a small, shallow dip in the snow, just a little too neat to be natural. "Wait. Look there."

Ashlyn followed his gaze and saw it too. It wasn't much, just a patch where the snow didn't sit quite right. But it was enough. They scrambled over, dropping to their knees, digging into the frozen ground with their gloved hands. It was slow going, frustratingly slow, and the cold seeped in deeper with each passing second.

"We're never getting through this," Ashlyn muttered, her breath coming out in sharp puffs of frustration.

And then the air shifted. This wasn't just the winter chill. This was something sharper, colder—unnatural. It crawled down Ashlyn's spine, and when she looked up, she saw him.

Andrew.

At first, he was barely there, just a flicker, a whisper of a figure in the moonlight. But then he took shape, solidifying bit by bit. He stood at the edge of the bushes, and he wasn't anything like the man Vera had been waiting for. His shoulders sagged, his face gaunt and worn down with the weight of everything he'd carried—or failed to carry. The regret hung around him like a heavy coat, and even in the faint light, Ashlyn could see it, clear as day.

Vera saw it too. Her lips parted, and for a moment, there was something soft in her expression, something broken. Her hands hovered in the space between them, trembling just enough to show that deep down, part of her still wanted to reach for him, even after everything.

"You said you'd come back," she whispered, her voice tight with years of waiting. "You promised me... and I waited."

Her voice cracked, and it was like the fog of confusion that had kept her here all these years suddenly lifted, replaced with something rawer. The weight of it all—the waiting, the hurt, the abandonment—settled over her, and Ashlyn could feel the sharp sting of it.

Vera's fingers twitched, curling inward as her face hardened. Whatever tenderness had been there a moment ago was gone, replaced by the anger she'd held onto for so long.

Andrew stepped forward, just a little, like he wanted to close the distance, to fix it. But Vera's eyes darkened, and that fury that had kept her tethered here for so long rose up again, burning hot and cold all at once. Her hands dropped to her sides, fists clenched.

She didn't say another word. She just turned and vanished into the shadows, gone as quickly as she had come.

Andrew's form flickered, his hand still outstretched, his voice thin and broken as he called after her. "Wait..."

But she was already gone.

CHAPTER NINE

All I Want for Christmas is Boo

"Oh, my Vera," Andrew whispered.

Andrew's manifestation was stronger than before, almost solid. Ashlyn heard him clear as day, and it seemed Sebastian did too, judging by his curious expression.

"It's to be expected, I'm afraid," Andrew said as his features relaxed, touched with sorrow. "This... this softening of the brain. I counted each month, watching for it to settle in fully, but I hoped the promise of our annual party would keep her spirits bright a while longer."

"She was not losing her mind, you know," Sebastian huffed.

"If she was so unwell, why on earth did you leave her alone?" Ashlyn added.

Andrew's back stiffened. "Alone?" he repeated, affronted. "No, I would never have left Vera alone. Annie was with her—my own cousin, and one of the very first to graduate from the nursing school! She was prepared for this, emotionally and practically."

Ashlyn pondered his words, but the puzzle still nagged at her. "Then why is Vera convinced Annie stole her money?"

Andrew's brows knitted in genuine confusion. "Annie? Never! When Vera's memory began to fail her, we were the ones who sponsored Annie through nursing school. We knew we'd need her help, and she was family. When we passed, the money would have gone to her anyway—no need for thievery."

Ashlyn could see the sincerity in Andrew's eyes, but he continued, almost as if speaking to himself. "No, Annie loved Vera, even as her mind unraveled... still, I knew what people might try to do if I couldn't come back. We hid our valuables, Vera and I, locked them away and buried them in the lilac garden. It was our way of keeping her safe if I didn't return in time, safe from the greedy sort who would take her away for their own gain."

"The asylum," Sebastian murmured.

Andrew nodded. "Precisely. That act was meant to protect her from the worst of what might come. Annie knew of it, of course. She would have been Vera's keeper. But if we truly have been dead these hundred years…" He trailed off, his face shadowed with loss.

Ashlyn watched as Andrew moved to the edge of the lilac bushes, reaching toward a spot he seemed to remember with absolute certainty. His hand wavered above the soil, fingers stretched as if he might feel the cold metal of the box beneath the earth. Ashlyn sensed that he was caught halfway between memory and reality.

"Aye, the strongbox," he murmured. "We buried it together, Vera and I. There's a key—a small, silver one with a lilac etched on the bow. I didn't want anyone else to find it, save Annie, who knew where to look if it came to that." He glanced at Ashlyn. "Vera's safety, her dignity… those were the things I valued more than gold."

Ashlyn could almost see him there, in another time, huddled over the turned soil, Vera beside him.

Andrew continued, almost speaking to himself. "I thought I would return by Christmas, you know. I only left to improve the curriculum, to make sure nurses knew what kindness looked like, how it felt in the hand." His gaze grew distant, fixed somewhere far away. "Our party was waiting. Our traditions..."

"Oh, my Vera," he whispered. "I never meant for this. I was the one to be alone. It was my cross to bear."

A silence followed, stretching long and thin. Ashlyn felt it, the loneliness of love bound by memory but broken by time.

Sebastian cleared his throat, glancing between Andrew and Ashlyn, his voice quieter than usual. "And without you, she passed, left to drift through the years, trapped in a Christmas that never came."

Andrew flinched, as if the memory itself had struck him. "Our Christmas—once filled with light—became nothing but fog and shadows for her."

Words tumbled around in Ashlyn's mind, but none seemed enough to touch the ache woven into Andrew's voice. She felt a pang herself, understanding that Vera—poor, stubborn, lost Vera—had clung to Christmas and to Andrew's promise as though they were her lifeline. But instead of saving her, they'd only served as an anchor, pulling her deeper into the darkness.

A flicker of resolve pierced through the grief in Andrew's eyes as he turned to Ashlyn. "Bring her here, to the garden," he said. "It was her joy, her haven. If anything can reach her, this place will."

Ashlyn exchanged a glance with Sebastian before they stepped away, leaving Andrew standing alone. As they walked back toward the house, his figure blended into the shadows of the garden, a solitary silhouette swallowed by the day.

"That was a little harsh, don't you think?" Ashlyn murmured, glancing sidelong at Sebastian. "Making him feel like Vera's heartbreak was his fault?"

Sebastian gave a noncommittal shrug. "It wasn't my intent to hurt his feelings," he replied. "But any path to resolution starts with the truth—and whether he knows it or not, I did him a service."

"Maybe you're right. But Vera... she's going to be a much harder nut to crack."

They scoured the house, weaving through Vera's usual haunts—the sitting room, the entryway, even the Lilac suite. Not a trace. At last, they found her in the attic, crouched in a shadowed corner like a wounded animal. Her rage hummed through the room as she tore into old clothing and furniture, her touch leaving a mess in her wake. To anyone who didn't know her sadness, the scene might have been terrifying.

"Vera," Ashlyn called. "Andrew never meant to leave you. He wanted to come home."

With a hollow gasp, Vera's face appeared inches from Ashlyn's own, her eyes dark with something almost feral. "He's dead to me," she spat, the words sharp as broken glass. Then she vanished back into the corner, ripping at the attic's contents, lost in her relentless loop.

Sebastian placed a gentle hand on her arm. "Unlike Andrew, she needs a softer touch. Let's give her a moment."

They retreated back downstairs, leaving the attic behind, and settled into the sitting room to gather their thoughts.

The house stayed quiet that morning. Ashlyn found herself lost in a book, and Sebastian settled in at the piano, fingers drifting over the keys. It was peaceful, a rare calm before the inevitable storm.

But when Delores and John arrived, the music faded, and Sebastian stood to greet them. They looked calm but quiet, a settled sort of acceptance in their eyes.

"How was the appointment?" Ashlyn asked.

Delores sighed. "As expected. Its confirmed, but I'm in the early stages. We've got a plan to slow things down, but..." She gave a shrug, her eyes meeting Ashlyn's. "It's a road I'll be traveling, like it or not."

"I'm so sorry." Ashlyn crossed the room and pulled Delores into a hug.

"Oh, don't worry about me, dear." Delores managed a small smile. "I'm all right, at least for now. How's our Vera?"

Ashlyn couldn't help but smile. "Quite a big step forward today."

She filled them in on Andrew's manifestation and Vera's own struggle with dementia.

"They called it a softening of the brain, or sometimes madness," she murmured.

"Well, I certainly feel a bit mad myself when I find I've-wandered into strange places," Delores said, chuckling.

Sebastian turned to John. "How are you holding up?"

John was quiet, his brow furrowing. "If I could trade places, I would," he said. "Dolly's always been the one with the gentle touch. The natural caretaker..."

"Oh, nonsense," Delores interrupted, giving him a reassuring squeeze. "Think of it as a role reversal! You'll do just fine."

Then her gaze shifted to Ashlyn, thoughtful. "Do you think...Vera would talk to me?"

Ashlyn looked over at Sebastian, who nodded. "She's had sometime to calm herself," he said. "It would be lovely to try."

They climbed to the attic in a quiet line, John helping Delores up the narrow stairs. Ashlyn brought the spirit box, figuring it was the easiest way to facilitate a conversation. If Vera was as loud as she'd been earlier, the box might not be necessary—but for those who couldn't hear the ghost, it made things simpler.

Setting up the box, Ashlyn tuned it to a low, steady static so Delores and John could hear. She explained how it worked, watching Delores's face shift with wonder.

"Vera," Sebastian called out. "This is Delores and John. They're the homeowners now. I believe you've met them?"

Vera's figure, still crouched in the far corner, lifted her head. Her gaze lingered on Delores and John, curiosity breaking through her sulking. She straightened, studying them.

"Is she here?" Delores asked.

Ashlyn gestured toward the corner, and Delores turned, her hand instinctively reaching out. John pulled a chair closer, guiding his wife to sit down.

"Thank you, John," Delores murmured as she settled in. The spirit box crackled, and Vera's voice came through, soft but distinct.

"Andrew was a gentleman."

Delores's eyes lit up. "She's here!" Her voice trembled, and for a moment, all of them fell silent.

Then Delores took a deep breath and began. "Hello, Vera. We've always loved having you here as part of our home. I hope you feel the same, sharing it with us and with our guests." She paused, glancing at Ashlyn and then back at the faint outline of Vera. "Today, I learned something that I think you and I share. I found out that I, too, have this... condition, this softening of the mind. And yes, I am scared. I don't want to fade away, to lose myself."

Vera watched her, the anger in her expression dimming to something more vulnerable.

Delores reached into her purse and pulled out a neatly folded piece of paper. "This is my care plan, Vera. I'm still well, and being with people I love, doing the things that bring me joy, that will slow the process." She smiled. "I want you to know that, even if they didn't understand it in your time, the work you and Andrew did—the kindness you showed—has helped people. And it will keep helping people."

Vera's figure seemed to flicker, the anger loosening around the edges. She drifted closer, and her voice whispered through the box.

"I don't want to slip away," Vera said, her words laced with longing. "I just... sometimes I don't know where I am anymore."

A tear slipped down Delores's cheek. "I know that feeling," she murmured. "But I've found a way to keep my feet grounded in the here and now, even if it's just one day at a time." She looked down at her plan. "And I hear you love Christmas and gardening. If you're around, I'd love to share those things with you—I love them too."

Vera's image grew clearer, the years of confusion lifting just a little. The walls she'd built to protect herself had begun to crumble. "I don't have to stay?"

As she spoke the words, a clarity washed over her face.

Delores smiled through her tears. "No, you don't. But if you do, know that we'd love to have you here. And if you go, know that we'll be happy for you, too."

For a moment, Vera looked around the room, truly seeing it—seeing all of them. Her shoulders relaxed, and a peace settled over her. "Thank you." The radio crackled.

"Will you come talk to Andrew?" Ashlyn asked.

Vera looked at Delores, then inclined her head.

Outside, the garden stood still and bare, frost clinging to the branches like delicate lace. Ashlyn, Sebastian, Delores, and John made their way into the clearing, moving through the brittle air. It felt heavy, almost expectant, as if the space itself was holding its breath, waiting for something to unfold.

Then Vera appeared. She was almost as clear as any of them; her form was steady in the winter light, her face softened in a way that seemed new. But her gaze went beyond, to where a figure waited under the frost-laden bushes.

Andrew stood, half in shadow, his eyes fixed on Vera as though he could hardly believe she was there. Vera drew closer, a little hesitantly, but then her hand reached out, curling around his. Her shoulders eased, the last of her anger falling away like autumn leaves.

"Andrew, you're—oh, you're here." Her voice sounded as if she were remembering herself for the first time in ages.

"Yes, my Vera." Andrew wrapped his arms around her, pulling her close, his face pressing into her hair. "I promised I'd come home for Christmas, didn't I?"

He leaned back and met her eyes, then looked toward the sky. "Shall we go, my love?"

Vera looked up, her gaze following his, the faintest shimmer of something just beyond their reach. The edges of her spirit seeming almost to blur in the cold air. But then she shook her head.

"One last Christmas, Andrew. With you," she whispered. She took his hand, her fingers lacing through his. "Let's stay and see it together."

Andrew touched her cheek. "Then one last Christmas it shall be." He looked over her shoulder, as if inviting everyone else into the thought. "We'll make it one to re-member."

Ashlyn felt the ache settle deep in her chest—a bitter-sweet pang, realizing how much this strange, found family had come to mean to her. She wasn't ready to let them go, not Vera or Andrew, or even the Millers with their quiet strength. There was something here, in this old garden and old house, something that bigger than herself. She wanted to keep it, even if it was just for a little longer.

Sebastian, sensing the thought in her gaze, laid a hand on her shoulder. "They'll stay through the holiday," he said, a smile in his voice as he looked over at John and Delores. "For one last celebration."

"Oh!" Delores clutched her hands together, her eyes wide with delight. "Vera will join us for Christmas! Isn't that something, John?"

John grinned, his face softening with relief. "Seems fit-ting, doesn't it?" He looked over at the garden, though he couldn't see what Ashlyn and Sebastian could. "She ought to have her Christmas."

Sebastian's eyes gleamed with a familiar spark, the one that meant he was about to cause trouble. "Well, then," he said, rubbing his hands together with an enthusiasm that felt almost contagious, "let's make it official. A Christmas party at Lilac Grove!" He paused, looking pointedly at

Ashlyn. "All of us. Together. With living, breathing people."

Delores lit up, clapping her hands. "Oh, yes! We'll bring in holly, ivy—maybe some candles! And mulled wine! And music!" She spun to John, eyes sparkling. "And maybe even a few guests?"

Ashlyn hesitated, surprised by the sudden enthusiasm. "Well, that all sounds lovely, but... I'm not sure who we'd even invite." She looked down, half-hoping the idea would fade if she didn't sound too interested. "I mean, most of my friends are, well, ghosts."

John's brow furrowed as he considered it, glancing at Delores as though she might have the answer. "Well, I suppose we'd want folks with, you know... an open mind. ""Exactly!" Delores nodded, warming to the idea. "People who would appreciate Lilac Grove's... unique charms."

"Unique charms?" Ashlyn repeated, giving a weak laugh. "You mean people who wouldn't run screaming if they met a ghost in the hall?"

"Oh, nonsense," Delores said, waving a hand. "We have plenty of friends who'd enjoy something a little unconventional! Don't we, John?"

John looked panicked, but nodded. "Certainly..."

Ashlyn shook her head. "I don't know, Delores. I'm not exactly the holiday hostess type."

"Oh, you'll be wonderful, dear," Delores said, dismissing Ashlyn's reluctance with a wave of her hand. "You don't have to do anything. Just leave it to us."

At that, Sebastian leaned in with a wicked grin. "I'll handle the invites." His eyes sparkled with a mischief that made Ashlyn nervous.

Ashlyn raised a wary eyebrow. "Sebastian, who exactly do you have in mind?"

"Oh, I have a few people," he said, his voice smooth, almost too innocent. "Consider it a surprise. You'll love them."

Delores gave a little gasp, clasping her hands. "Oh, I do love a surprise! And Ashlyn, just think—friends to help celebrate!."

Ashlyn bit her lip, realizing the warm feeling in her chest was, indeed, creeping up again. Friends who understood. Family, even, in a way that was unexpected but no less real. She tried to brush it off with a small shrug. "Fine," she muttered, half-smiling.

Sebastian chuckled. "Oh, just you wait. I guarantee this will be a Christmas to remember."

CHAPTER TEN

Auld Lang Syne

It was Christmas Eve, and the night of the party. Ashlyn stood in front of the mirror, tugging at the hem of a dress she hadn't worn in years. It was a deep burgundy, with just enough shimmer to catch the light, but not so much that it screamed holiday office party. She had tucked it into her suitcase just in case, and was glad she did.

She adjusted the neckline, tilting her head to one side as she inspected her reflection. If this didn't make her look like a responsible adult who was going to a real grown-up party, she didn't know what would. The sleeves felt restrictive, as if the dress could sense she usually lived in flowy skirts and long shirts. There, all set, she thought, giving herself one last once-over. Now she just needed a glass of something festive, and she will be ready to pretend she was having the time of her life.

Normally, she'd be at home. The past couple of years, that meant sharing the evening with Hank, her silent housemate. Part of her liked it that way—no holiday stress, no big dinners to cook or clean up after, just her, a warm blanket, and a few Christmas movies playing on loop. She could skip all the obligatory cheer and keep her holiday spirit at a low simmer, which was about as festive as she ever felt comfortable being.

Sebastian, on the other hand, had a sister with two little girls who adored him. Every year, he'd spend the season with them, spoiling them with gifts and, according to him, instigating a little chaos. In fact, he was leaving early tomorrow morning to make it to Christmas dinner with his nieces.

Ashlyn sometimes received invitations from clients or people she'd worked with, usually phrased in that polite, cautious way that suggested they were more curious about her than genuinely interested. "Do you have plans for the holidays, Ashlyn? You're more than welcome to join us." She could hear the unspoken questions behind their words, and she always politely declined. She wasn't sure if they thought she was lonely, or if they were just trying to learn more about her home life, but it never felt quite right to accept.

On a typical Christmas Day, she'd make herself a quiet breakfast, sit by the window, and reflect. She wondered how many other people spent the holidays alone. Were they lonely, or was it a choice? Society had placed such a heavy weight on this season, and she had learned to embrace the quiet moments, to find comfort in them.

There was always a little sadness for what could have been. What might have been. Who would she be if her parents were still around? If she hadn't been shuffled from one foster home to another? She liked who she was now. She really did. She'd built a life, a strange and sometimes transient one, but hers all the same. And she wouldn't change it.

But, the thought of an alternate version of herself, one who had a family that wasn't made up of ghosts, was... intriguing. Would she pity the version of herself who spent Christmas alone, or would she be envious of the peace and freedom that came with it?

Ashlyn shook her head, smiling at her reflection. "Alright, enough of that," she said, smoothing the front of her dress one last time. "Let's go do this." She gave herself a wink in the mirror. "Happy Christmas to me."

The Millers and Sebastian were already gathered downstairs. Ashlyn hesitated at the top step, taking a deep breath before making her way down. She could smell warm cider and freshly baked gingerbread, mingling with the faint hint of pine. As she descended, she heard Sebastian's voice, teasing.

"Fashionably late, darling," he called, flashing her a grin as she appeared. "I love it."

"How can I be late if no one else has arrived?" she shot back, lifting an eyebrow as she took in the scene.

"You're the last one to our party," he replied as he handed her a glass of merlot. "Which, technically, still makes you late."

Ashlyn accepted the glass. "At least I'm worth the wait."

Sebastian laughed. "Always."

He looked spectacular tonight, dressed in a midnight blue suit that complimented his silver hair. He'd added a crimson pocket square that matched his signature scarf, and the whole effect was striking—like he'd stepped out of a magazine ad for expensive cologne.

Ashlyn turned her attention to the rest of the room, and her breath caught. Delores and John had outdone themselves. The large tree in the entryway, already impressive, now seemed to glow from within, strung with hundreds of tiny white lights that winked like stars. Ornaments in shades of gold and red hung from every branch, catching the light and casting a kaleidoscope of colors across the room.

Vera had been quiet over the past week, no tantrums or outbursts. Ashlyn suspected that having Andrew's spirit by her side had calmed her. Still, she had made her presence known, poking her head around now and then to supervise.

The Millers were standing by the fireplace, their hands intertwined. Delores looked radiant in a red, sparkly dress that shimmered every time she moved. John was wearing a deep red tie that matched her dress, his dark suit a subtle, classic counterpoint to Delores's shine. It was perfect—he was her grounding force.

"This place looks spectacular," Ashlyn said, her voice full of awe. "I mean, it was already gorgeous, but now it's… it's like a magazine spread come to life."

Delores beamed. "Oh, thank you, dear. We wanted it to feel special, you know? Like a proper celebration."

"And here's to you, Ashlyn." Sebastian clinked his glass against hers. "You've been a busy little elf this month, keeping the peace and solving mysteries. I think we can all agree. We wouldn't be here without you."

Ashlyn blushed. "I didn't do that much."

"Oh, hush," Delores said, stepping forward to pull Ashlyn into a hug, her sequins catching the light and sparkling even more. "You did more than you know. This whole place feels... lighter. Happier. That's because of you."

Ashlyn felt a lump form in her throat, and she took a sip of her wine to swallow it down. "Well, if I'm going to keep getting compliments, I'm going to need more of this," she said, raising her glass with a grin.

John chuckled and nodded toward the bar. "Plenty more where that came from. Help yourself."

They were interrupted by the chime of the doorbell. Okay, game face, Ashlyn told herself, setting down her glass and straightening her dress. She glanced up at the banister as John moved to answer the door.

There, at the top of the stairs, stood Andrew and Vera, side by side, like royalty, looking down on their subjects. They were radiant, their faces alight with a joy that seemed to belong to a different time, a different world.

Andrew was dressed in a tailored black tailcoat, his white shirt crisp with a high, starched collar. Beneath, a deep green vest embroidered with gold filigree glimmered in the light. He looked every inch the gentleman.

It was Vera who dazzled. Her gown, a rich burgundy velvet with black lace that traced delicate patterns along the bodice and sleeves. The modest neckline framed a string of pearls that rested against her throat. The dress cinched at her waist, flaring out into a sweeping skirt that seemed to float as she moved. Long satin gloves reached past her elbows, and her hair was styled in a loose, elegant chignon, with a few soft curls framing her face.

They looked as if they had stepped out of a vintage portrait, composed and timeless. For a moment, Ashlyn could hardly believe they were spirits—there was such vitality in the way they stood, shoulders almost touching, like a couple who had spent a lifetime together. It was hard to imagine the sadness and restlessness that had haunted Vera, seeing her now, so poised and graceful.

Ashlyn turned back to the door, squinting at the couple standing on the threshold. The man was tall with sandy blond hair, and the woman beside him had chestnut hair that framed her face—and a very noticeable baby bump.

"Oh my goodness!" Ashlyn squealed, her usual composure slipping. "The Hartley's!"

She had worked with Benjamin years ago, back when she was consulting for a TV show investigating paranormal sites. Misthaven Light had been one of her earliest mysteries, and it was during that case that Benjamin had met his wife, Ella. Ashlyn liked to think she had played a small part in bringing them together.

She rushed forward to greet them, her arms already outstretched. "Ella! Benjamin! It's been ages! Look at you—glowing, both of you!"

Ella beamed, her cheeks flushed with happiness, and she patted her rounded belly. "We're doing great, Ashlyn. I'm still painting, and people are buying my postcards like crazy."

"They've clearly got excellent taste," Ashlyn said, grinning. "And you, Benjamin? Still neck-deep in dusty old records?"

Benjamin chuckled. "Guilty as charged. I've actually been promoted—head of the Maine Historical Society. And I published that book on lighthouse history. It's even got a chapter about Misthaven Light."

"Oh, that's wonderful!" Ashlyn clapped her hands together.

"Turns out there's a whole world of people out there who want to know the gruesome details of shipwrecks and haunted beacons," Benjamin said. "Who knew?"

"And the baby?" Ashlyn asked as she glanced at Ella's belly. "Do we have a name picked out yet?"

Ella and Benjamin exchanged a look, a silent conversation passing between them. "We're thinking of 'Margot,'" she said. "It was the name of Benjamin's favorite great-aunt. She was a bit of a legend in the family, so it just... feels right."

Ashlyn's eyes softened. "I'm so happy for both of you."

They chatted a little longer, catching up on old times, and Ashlyn marveled at how life had changed for the Hartley's. They were both thriving, with a family of their own on the way.

While Ashlyn had been catching up, the room had filled. She glanced around, her eyes scanning the crowd and taking in so many familiar faces, each one bright with holiday cheer. It felt like a reunion of sorts, a gathering of people who had, in one way or another, become part of her life.

"Did you organize all this, Seb?" she asked, turning to Sebastian, who was sipping a glass of something festive.

"It was easy," he replied, grinning. "Everyone loves you so much."

Ashlyn's heart gave a happy flutter at that. Before she could respond, her eyes landed on another couple she recognized.

Clara and Jack stood nearby, and Clara's face lit up the moment she spotted Ashlyn. In her hands, she held a neatly wrapped book, tied with a ribbon that had a tiny sprig of holly tucked into it.

"Ashlyn!" Clara beamed. "I have something for you." She held out the package, and Ashlyn took it. "It's a signed copy of my latest! I couldn't have finished it without your help on all the spooky details, so... Merry Christmas."

"You didn't have to do that—but thank you! I'm so proud of you. Another bestseller on the way, I'm sure."

Clara blushed, waving off the praise. "Well, let's hope. We're still living with those Boston rents, so I'd better keep writing."

Ashlyn laughed, but then her eyes flicked to Jack, who seemed a little more fidgety than usual. His hand kept slipping into his pocket, as though he were double-checking something important. Curious, she tilted her head, but before she could ask if everything was alright, Sebastian nudged her.

Ashlyn followed his gaze, watching as Jack lead Clara toward the hearth. A few others gathered around, sensing that something special was unfolding. Jack, looking slightly nervous, took a deep breath and then, without another word, dropped to one knee.

"Clara," Jack began, his voice a little shaky, "you make every day brighter and more chaotic and... well, wonderful. I can't imagine life without you, and I don't want to." He pulled a small velvet box from his pocket and opened it, revealing a simple yet elegant ring that sparkled in the firelight. "Will you marry me?"

For a heartbeat, the room was silent. Then Clara gasped, and she threw her arms around Jack, nearly knocking him over in her eagerness. "Yes! Of course, yes!" she managed.

The room erupted into applause and cheers. Ashlyn clapped along.

"Looks like it's not just ghosts finding happiness tonight," Sebastian whispered, leaning close so only she could hear. "There's some love for the living, too."

The applause for Clara and Jack's engagement settled, though Ashlyn could still hear bursts of laughter and excited chatter echoing through the room. She backed away from the cluster of well-wishers, feeling a pleasant hum of happiness that wasn't her own. It was nice, this kind of joy—she wasn't used to it, but she found she didn't mind.

Her stomach growled, reminding her she had skipped lunch. She turned to head towards the refreshment table, intent on locating whatever remained of the cheese platter, when she caught sight of a pair of familiar faces huddled together near the fireplace. Sienna Avery and Nora Sinclar were leaning in close, talking. Ashlyn's curiosity sparked; she hadn't known they even knew each other.

As she got closer, she caught the tail end of their conversation.

"—since high school, can you believe it?" Sienna was saying, her eyes wide with excitement. "I still can't get over it. You look exactly the same!"

Nora laughed, tossing her head back. She caught sight of Ashlyn approaching and grinned. "And look who it is—the woman who seems to know everyone, everywhere."

Ashlyn smiled back, slipping between them. "Hey, I didn't realize this was a reunion. Do I need to break out the yearbooks?"

Sienna gave a little hop, still glowing. "We went to high school together! And we haven't seen each other since... well, graduation, I think. This is so wild."

"Small world, isn't it?" She glanced between them. "So, what have you been catching up on? I need updates too!"

"Oh, all the usual things," Nora said, waving a hand. "School, work, how life makes no sense, but we're all trying to pretend it does. Sienna's about to graduate from Plymouth State. Can you believe it?"

"It's true!" Sienna said. "I'm finally finishing my degree this spring. And I've been working with Dylan on the rebrand of White Pines Resort."

"That's brilliant, Sienna. I knew the two of you make it happen."

"He's been amazing," Sienna said. "Handling all the business-y stuff, which is great because I'm terrible at it. I am doing marketing, blogs articles and such. It's nice, you know? Working together is so special."

Nora arched an eyebrow. "You're not alone there. I've been in a similar boat—except my boat has more drama and people forgetting their lines." She turned to Ashlyn. "Alex's play is getting a second run."

"No way! That's fantastic. They are so talented. You both are. "

"Yep," Nora said, sounding equal parts proud and amused. "Alex has been so supportive. We've got this weird, lovely little creative partnership going on."

"Just creative?" Ashlyn teased. "I'm sure it's a little more than just a creative partnership. You two were pretty close. Last I checked."

Nora blushed.. "We just... fit. Anyway, we'd love to have you come to the show. You were there for the first one; it feels right that you're there for this one, too."

"I wouldn't miss it," Ashlyn said, and meant it.

"Well," Sienna said, glancing around, "I should probably find Dylan before he gets himself in trouble. But I'm so glad we got to do this, Nora. We need to catch up more often."

"We will," Nora said. "And you, Ashlyn—don't disappear before I have time to corner you about the show dates. Plus, Alex will want to say hi."

Ashlyn smiled, feeling something small and warm nestle itself in her heart. "I'll be here."

As Ashlyn stood surveying the crowd, she spotted Vera near the fireplace, her form mingling almost naturally among the living guests. The ghost's presence was subtle—a flicker at the edge of the twinkling lights, a faint wisp of breath that misted the air. Vera seemed content, watching the festivities with an air of nostalgia.

"Having fun?" came a voice beside her.

Ashlyn turned to see Sebastian.

"More than expected," she replied.

The evening wound down, and the room settled into that cozy, sleepy calm that comes after too much wine and just the right amount of merriment. Conversations softened into murmurs, and the last of the guests began pulling on their coats, clutching leftover cookies wrapped in napkins, and making all the vague, well-meaning promises people make at the end of a party.

It was well past midnight by the time the last guests trickled out, leaving the house quiet and warm. Over by the fireplace, the Millers were engaged in a playful debate about whether John would need to shovel the walk again in the morning. Delores, hands on her hips, informed him that if it snowed tonight, she'd drag him back inside by his ear. "No work tomorrow," she declared, a mock sternness in her tone. Ashlyn smiled, feeling a familiar warmth settle over her.

From across the room, Sebastian caught her eye, his shoes clicking softly on the floor as he made his way over. "Happy Christmas, all!" he announced, glancing at his watch with a playful flourish.

"And to you," Ashlyn replied, her voice light. Delores added a more enthusiastic, "Merry Christmas, Sebastian!" as she beamed at him.

"Well, darlings," he said, his grin softer than usual, "I think it's time I made my exit to bed. I need to leave absurdly early tomorrow if I want to make it home for Christmas morning with my nieces. They'd have my head if I missed it. And probably try to put tinsel on it."

Ashlyn sighed, wishing he could stay up a bit longer, but she managed a smile. "I wouldn't dream of getting between you and your tiny, tinsel-wielding tyrants. Besides, you've got a long trip ahead. You'll need your beauty rest."

"Is that code for, 'You need to go to bed, old man?'" he teased, narrowing his eyes. Then he pulled her into a hug, squeezing just a bit tighter than usual. "Thank you,

Ashlyn. For everything. This was... a strange and lovely kind of Christmas."

As he spoke, Ashlyn's gaze drifted to the staircase, where she saw them—Vera and Andrew, standing side by side at the banister, looking down at the quiet room below. They were almost glowing, their forms shimmering with a soft, ethereal light that seemed to pulse gently, like a heartbeat. The glow brightened, intensifying until it was almost blinding. Then, just as quickly, it began to break apart, dispersing into a million tiny stars that drifted upward, fading like embers on a dark night.

"That was beautiful," Sebastian whispered.

Ashlyn blinked away a tear that had stubbornly formed at the corner of her eye. "I don't think we'll see them again," she said.

Sebastian nodded, his expression tender. "I'm glad they found peace." He slipped an arm around her shoulders and gave a comforting squeeze. "Thank you for inviting me, darling. This has been a Christmas miracle."

Ashlyn hugged him back, holding on just a little longer than usual. "I'm glad I got to share this moment with you, my dear friend."

"Likewise," he said. "Now, I really must get a good night's sleep before I'm buried under a pile of Christmas bows and overexcited children."

He gave a final, exaggerated salute to John and Delores, who waved back like they were seeing off royalty. Then, with a swirl of his scarf, he was gone.

Without Sebastian, the room felt emptier. As the fire crackled and the lights blinked, she could hear the creak of the old house settling, like it was sighing into sleep.

"Well," Delores said, breaking the silence, "I suppose we should turn in too. I've got to make a feast tomorrow, and John's going to need all his strength if he plans on finishing the last of the pies."

"I'm saving room," John said with a sage nod, then gave Ashlyn a serious look. "We're planning on having a proper hunt for that old strongbox come spring when the ground melts."

"It's more curiosity than anything, really." Delores added. "Just a little mystery left over, like a puzzle piece." Then she reached out and took Ashlyn's hands in hers. "You'll have to come back in the spring and see if we find it."

"Oh, I'll be back," Ashlyn replied. "I'm far too curious to stay away."

John chuckled, gave her a firm handshake, then turned toward the door.

"Goodnight, Ashlyn," Delores said, letting go of her hands. "Merry Christmas. And thank you for everything you've done."

Ashlyn followed them and watched from the porch as John and Delores made their way home, arm in arm, their laughter drifting through the still night. She felt a quiet contentment settle over her. The night had been perfect—not because she loved parties, but because of the wonderful people that had touched her life over the years.

Then she stepped back inside. The fire had burned low, leaving just a few glowing embers that pulsed like stars that weren't quite ready to fade. She stood there for a moment and let herself savor the peace. She had spent years on her own, drifting through towns, solving mysteries that no one else could see, but something was different now. For the first time in a long while, she didn't feel like a visitor passing through. Maybe that was what finding your place was—realizing that home could be a collection of mismatched moments, with people who didn't need to be asked to stay.

She let her voice drift into the stillness, a simple blessing, before turning to go upstairs. "Merry Christmas."

Also by

ALSO BY BETH CONNOR:

Hollow City

<u>The Isdralan Chronicles:</u>
Micah and the Candles of Time
Prodigy of Flame
Bridge of Blood and Thornes

<u>Kindred Spirit Mysteries:</u>
The Secret of Misthaven Island
Bridging the Heart
The Curse at White Pines

The Last Act

About the Author

B eth Connor is a weaver of tales, captivated by writing and fueled by a love for storytelling.

Beth's creative pursuits are a reflection of her life philosophy, and she is always searching for new ways to expand her knowledge and understanding of the world. She has a keen eye for detail and a remarkable ability to create vivid, dynamic settings that resonate with her audience.

Beth's talent has earned her recognition as the author of several published works, including the novel "Hollow City" The Isdralan Chronicles Series, and the Kindred Spirits Mysteries, as well as a contributor to many anthologies. Beth is also an accomplished audiobook narrator and the host of the popular podcast, "Crossroads Cantina."

Despite her many endeavors, Beth remains down-to-earth and dedicated to living authentically, true to her passions and values. She resides in the Pacific Northwest with her husband, two children, and canine companions, who bring her boundless inspiration and delight.